# UNVEILING A PARALLEL

UTOPIANISM AND COMMUNITARIANISM
Lyman Tower Sargent and Gregory Claeys
*Series Editors*

# UNVEILING A PARALLEL

## A ROMANCE

ALICE ILGENFRITZ JONES

ELLA MERCHANT

(Two Women of the West)

With an Introduction by
Carol A. Kolmerten

"The awful lines of space are thrilling indeed,
when there is a world at each end."—DAVID SWING

SYRACUSE UNIVERSITY PRESS

Copyright © 1991 by Syracuse University Press
Syracuse, New York 13244-5160

Syracuse University Press Edition 1991
05  06  07  08  09  10        7  6  5  4  3  2

This book was originally published in 1893 by Arena Publishing Company.

The paper used in this publication meets the minimum requirements of American National Standard for Information Sciences — Permanence of Paper for Printed Library Materials, ANSI Z39.48-1984. ∞™

**Library of Congress Cataloging-in-Publication Data**

Two women of the West.
    Unveiling a parallel : a romance / Alice Ilgenfritz Jones, Ella Merchant ; with an introduction by Carol A. Kolmerten.
        p.    cm. — (Utopianism and communitarianism)
    ISBN 0-8156-2538-3. — ISBN 0-8156-0259-6 (pbk.)
    I. Title.    II. Series.
PS991.A6U58    1991
813'.4 — dc20                                                91-19577
                                                               CIP

# CONTENTS

CAROL A. KOLMERTEN is Professor of English at Hood College. She is the author of *Women in Utopia: The Ideology of Gender in the American Owenite Communities* and editor of *Utopus Discovered,* the newsletter of the Society for Utopian Studies.

# ACKNOWLEDGMENTS

I always wanted to be a detective. Like so many prepubescent girls, I read about Nancy Drew avidly, progressing to C. Auguste Dupin and Nero Wolfe. I was always particularly impressed with the classical detectives — the kind who could sit back in their very easy chairs and think of the solution, while everyone else ran around finding clues, but not putting the whole picture together. I have discovered in this project that, while classical detectives may make good reading for adolescent minds, they are purely fictional constructs.

Before I could write this introduction, I had to play detective and what I learned is that I would never have found out anything without luck and without help from a multitude of people. Luck, not skill, is the most important element in solving any mystery and so it was in my case. Had I not asked to see the Curator of Rare Books while I was doing research on another project at the Houghton, I might never have met Roger Stoddard, who probably knows more about Arena Publishing Company than any other living person. When I asked him if he had any idea of where Alice Ilgenfritz Jones and Ella Merchant had lived, my request took him to an old box of Arena notes where he found a Cedar Rapids address for the authors. With that information, I was able to begin.

The person who has supplied me with the vital information about the lives of Jones and Merchant is Marilyn J. Walsh, the president of the Linn County Heritage Society in Cedar Rapids, Iowa. Ms. Walsh uncovered obituaries, cemetery listings, and reviews. Without Ms. Walsh's tireless assistance, I could not have written this introduction.

Once I had gathered information about the unknown authors, I received considerable and astute comments from four of the most respected scholars working with nineteenth-century utopian literature: Kenneth Roemer, Carol Farley Kessler, Jean Pfaelzer, and Lyman Tower Sargent. Their suggestions helped me immeasurably.

Syracuse University Press has made writing this introduction as effortless as possible; and I would also like to thank the press staff, who helped to make this book a reality.

As always, I owe my greatest debt to my colleague and spouse, Stephen M. Ross. Not only did Steve read many drafts and offer his usual excellent editorial commentary, but he also helped me battle recalcitrant printers and obsolete software commands.

I thank finally the people and resources of Hood College, but particularly the students who made up English 310 in the spring of 1990. They inspired me then and continue to inspire me with their wit and their search to open the canon to a book like this one. It is for them that these words written a hundred years ago need to be printed again.

# INTRODUCTION

In 1893, two "Women of the West" who lived in Cedar Rapids, Iowa, sent their book to Arena Publishing Company in Boston, a press that specialized in works of social reform. Editor Benjamin O. Flower liked the book; and by the summer of 1893 the collaborative effort, *Unveiling a Parallel*, was released for one dollar hardbound, fifty cents paperback. The following year it came out in a second edition and then quietly went out of print.

The book was not reviewed in mainstream magazines such as *Lippincott's Monthly Magazine* or the *Atlantic Monthly*, probably because of Arena's reputation as a minor press for radicals and authors who paid to see their books published. Yet, when *Parallel* was reviewed, it received praise along with some misunderstanding. One reviewer in the *Kansas City Journal* lauded the Two Women of the West for their boldness of diction and completeness of argument, while a reviewer from the *Toledo Saturday Blade* pronounced the book "one of the keenest of satires upon existing social and political conditions on earth. It 'unveils a parallel' most truly, and in so doing, turns a search light upon some of the myths which have been accepted as gospel truths bearing upon the relations of men and women to each other. It is amusing, interesting and suggestive, and most decidedly worth a reading." The editor of the *Cedar Rapids Evening Gazette* understood that the "gist of the . . . book is that there should be but one moral code for men and women alike." This editor wrote that the book possessed unusual character and individuality and "promises to be a distinct literary success." Other reviewers were not as positive, with one man so exasperated with the authors "forget[ting]" to name the narrator that he called him "Peter." This reviewer found some of the customs of Mars "very nice" but questioned whether they were an improvement over "the good old sparkling days they have enjoyed on this planet, and especially out West."[1]

For almost a hundred years, *Unveiling a Parallel* has remained out of print, with few extant copies. The women who wrote the book, Alice Ilgenfritz Jones and Ella Merchant, are unknown to all but scholars in utopian studies, though Alice was a novelist and travel writer of some repute in turn-of-the-century America. The few literary biographies and bibliographies that do include Alice I. Jones incorrectly cite her as a Louisiana author.[2] The Library of Congress author cards record no dates for Ella Merchant's birth or death and only note Alice Jones's death in 1906. These women have remained lost writers, their book doomed to an unjustified obscurity.

*Unveiling a Parallel,* despite its obscurity, is one of the most clever and humorous of novels published in late nineteenth-century America. Whether we label it a utopian novel, a sentimental romance, an astute satire of the limitations of late nineteenth-century gender roles and "proper" spheres for women, or a feminist novel ahead of its time is inconsequential because the book is all of these things and more. Within its 269 pages, its two obscure authors uncover a plethora of parallels between the earth of their day and the Mars of their imaginations.

### The Lives of Ella Merchant and Alice Ilgenfritz Jones

If we can believe the generalizations of history books, the early 1890s were turbulent, fraught with the "panic of '93" and a subsequent depression. We read, on one hand, of a "gilded age" and the making of great fortunes; we read, on the other hand, of the effect of these great fortunes on the working class and the concomitant reform movements including the Single Tax, the Nationalist clubs, and the Progressive party. Some women were writing and speaking for suffrage and for other important reforms including temperance and child labor. Other women were involved in a "Social Hygiene" movement, which emphasized improving health and moral self-control.[3] Yet others were attracted to the Social Gospel movement, with its underlying evangelical and spiritual responses to the evils of "modern" living.

What the depression and the era's reform movements meant to residents of Cedar Rapids, Iowa, we cannot know with certainty. Advertisements for Franco-American soups, Ivory soap, and Bissell's carpet sweepers filled the pages of the popular magazines that residents of Cedar Rapids read. Pictures of corsets illustrated what middle-class women should look like. Essays on "torpid liver problems" suggested that constipation caused a variety of ills from sick headaches to dyspepsia. The *Atlantic Monthly* reviewed new editions of Henry James's "Daisy Miller" and Hawthorne's "Wonder Book." Whittier's poems graced every popular monthly. Arthur Conan Doyle's short stories proliferated in a number of magazines, and the sentimental romance remained a popular favorite among many readers.

At the time their book was published, Alice Ilgenfritz Jones and Ella Merchant led in many ways quite typical upper middle-class lives as wives of a part owner of the Jones and Luberger

Furniture Company and the business manager of the Republican Printing Company respectively. Born Ella Robinson on September 26, 1857, Ella Merchant was a native of Iowa. Her parents had moved to Iowa from New York in 1856, settling near Des Moines. Her father, William Robinson, was a physician who served in the Civil War and then returned to his practice in Cedar Falls until his death in 1885. Ella married L. Stoddard Merchant in 1877. Lorenzo Merchant, like Ella's father, had grown up in New York and then left the East when he was twenty to seek his fortune in Iowa. He became involved with a variety of newspapers and printing companies. Lorenzo Merchant died in 1894, the year the second edition of *Unveiling a Parallel* was issued. Ella became president of his printing company the following year. The editor of the *Cedar Rapids Evening Gazette* writes that Ella had "never done any independent literary work" before her coauthorship of *Unveiling a Parallel* but was known as an "exceedingly clever woman" (June 3, 1893). Ella died on June 16, 1916, in Lincoln, Nebraska, probably childless, as her obituary did not name any children.[4]

Eleven years older than Ella, Alice Ilgenfritz was born in Ohio in 1846 but lived most of her life in Cedar Rapids. Alice's father, Harry Ilgenfritz, married her mother, Anna Murray, in 1843 in Ohio. In 1863, they moved to Iowa and settled at Clarksville, where Harry became a furniture dealer and eventually mayor of the city, while serving on the school board for sixteen years. Alice, educated at Evansville Seminary in Wisconsin, wrote her first book under the pseudonym Ferris Jerome. *High-Water-Mark*, published by J. B. Lippincott and Company in 1879, was a sentimental romance written within the conventions of its era. The protagonist, a poetry-writing young man by the name of Charles Burns, is a sensitive soul who has nonetheless committed an unpardonable sin of breaking his engagement. Burns spends most of his narrative time in a melancholy trance, regretting his rash action. The heroine of the book, Wilmagard Lynne, is a sprightly, well-intentioned young woman whose only sin is not being quite as beautiful or as well born as the elegant Maude MacIvers, the woman whose presence convinces Burns that he no longer loves Wilma. Wilma, because she could not marry the man she loved, reached her "highest possibilities" (382) when she had to learn to live an independent life. Yet, despite Wilma's worldly success as an elocutionist, she must live her life without love, as must Charles. In a conventional ending, Wilma dies and Charles pines away, forever doomed to unhappiness because he could not realize the worth of the woman who loved him. Although Wilma does die, her moral superiority allows her a kind of martyrdom.

During the early 1880s, Alice Ilgenfritz continued to write, primarily short pieces of fiction and travel essays, for *Lippincott's Monthly Magazine*. One of her short stories for *Lippincott's*, "Westbrook" (August 1880), is a reworking of *High-Water-Mark* that was bound to please its female readers. In "Westbrook," the heroine retained her moral authority but married as well. "Westbrook"'s main character, Ruth Stanley, is a dedicated teacher, engaged to the town's young doctor. Her foil, a Miss Custer, is a well-dressed belle who is out to win the good doctor away from Ruth. As in *High-Water-Mark*, the good woman loses her man to this less worthy woman. But in "Westbrook," the town's other single man, a lawyer, proposes to Ruth; she then ends up living in Westbrook's most elegant home. Her former fiancé neglects his business, and her foil is known throughout the town as a lazy and shiftless woman.

Alice also wrote travel essays, documenting her journeys on "The Lakes of Minnesota" or traveling "Down the Red River of the North." This kind of essay, with its weaving of historical back-

ground, descriptions of strange peoples, and sketches of unex-
plored territories, was immensely popular with readers of such
magazines as *Lippincott's,* perhaps for the same reasons that the
sentimental romance was. The subtext underlying the descriptions of flora and fauna of Minnesota or Manitoba told readers
how to behave—what to do with one's time and money—and must
have appealed, particularly, to the newly rich or the rising middle class. Alice writes of a life of upper middle-class leisure, of
days of drinking lemonade with friends: "I could not resist the
impulse, after the little company had dispersed and gone to drink
lemonade in the pavilion on the lawn, to steal back and stand
alone in the presence of the Laughing Water; for it has a presence. Standing thus until the whole being—the imagination as
well as the senses—is intoxicated with its charm, one realizes how
far it is beyond description" ("The Lakes of Minnesota," 269).
The traces of meaning associated with drinking lemonade in pa-
vilions on lawns conjures up a calm, refined elegance. Unlike
the fictional Daisy Miller who dies because she does not behave
properly as a woman with new money, Alice Ilgenfritz tells her
readers, obliquely of course, just how to behave.

In 1884, Alice married for the first time at the age of thirty-
eight. Her husband, Hiram Edgar Jones, was a furniture dealer
like her father and a widower with a small daughter, Isabelle.
Becoming wife and mother in one ceremony, Alice Ilgenfritz
Jones's writing career virtually stopped from 1884 until she co-
authored *Parallel* in 1893. She then published *Beatrice of Bayou Teche*
in 1895 and *The Chevalier de St. Denis* in 1900.

Both *Beatrice* and *St. Denis* fit into the sentimental-historical
romance mold that shaped *High-Water-Mark. Beatrice* is the story
of a young woman who, though she looks white, is black. Set

primarily in New Orleans and the Louisiana Bayou country before the Civil War, *Beatrice* dealt with a familiar theme in sentimental romances — the beautiful mulatto, who, though her blood might be "impure," possessed a purer heart than the whites surrounding her. Beatrice, in the course of the novel, falls in love with her white cousin Burgoyne, who marries Helen, Beatrice's foil. Whereas Beatrice has a "spiritual force" (143), Helen writes trashy sentimental letters; whereas Beatrice is one with nature and animals, Helen wants to capture birds.

The novel details life before the Civil War in New Orleans and the Bayou country, a part of the country that Alice was well familiar with, as she often spent winters in Jennings, Louisiana, with her sister. One contemporary reviewer of the book complained that it used "beguiling local color" but the characters "travel everlastingly and the shifting of scenes reveal [*sic*] the weakness of the untutored novelist."[5]

In tying together her story lines, Alice follows the conventional plot twists of the sentimental novel. Helen, Beatrice's foil, drowns herself when she discovers that her husband loves Beatrice. Burgoyne is conveniently killed in the Civil War so that the subject of an interracial marriage will never have to be broached. Beatrice is allowed to live, but only as a single woman working as a missionary. Having been advised by her mentor, an older woman, to set herself up as an example for "the weaker ones of your race" (324), Beatrice, at the end of the book, is living on a remote island where the races mingle. She finds her life's work in painting and helping the natives.

In *The Chevalier de St. Denis,* Alice returns to a male protagonist, based on a hero in Louisiana history. *The Chevalier,* a historical romance, focuses on St. Denis who is twenty years old in 1710, the year in which the book begins. Slow-moving in its first 188 pages, set in France and Spain, among court intrigues and false incarcerations, the book picks up tempo when, in 1714, the setting shifts to Alabama, Louisiana, and Texas. Throughout a series of picaresque adventures, St. Denis remains faithful to his true love, Maria, whom he finally marries on the last page of the book. Maria has made this reunion possible by lying and deceiving her other suitor, the evil Gaspardo, who has imprisoned St. Denis. Because of Maria's clever plan, St. Denis is rescued from certain death and will prosper while Gaspardo's fortunes will fall as he, himself, is imprisoned.

After the publication of this last novel in 1900, by the reputable A. C. McClurg and Company in Chicago, who had also published *Beatrice,* Alice received a number of favorable reviews, as she had for *Beatrice.* [6] Her health failed somewhat, according to newspaper reports, though she continued to write more essays on her travels throughout California and the West. She died unexpectedly of a cerebral hemorrhage on March 5, 1906, in Havana, Cuba, where she and her husband had been vacationing for the previous six weeks. Her death, according to her obituary, caused "a shock of sadness to many hearts in the city, in the state, and in many other cities" because of her extensive traveling and authorship. But the obituary writer quickly pointed out that she had been "much more than a literary woman." She was, in accord with Cedar Rapids mores of the early twentieth century, "a notable home-maker and housekeeper and her hospitality was perfect in cordiality and friendliness." Though she had had "a strong nature," she was nonetheless "very true in [her] friendships and her cultivated mind made her a charming companion," She had also been "the kindest of mothers and the best of friends" to her step-daughter, Isabelle. [7]

## The Book

*Unveiling a Parallel* is a book about the absurdities connected with the social construction of "femaleness" and "maleness" in late nineteenth-century North America. It has been called a gender-role reversal, a utopia stressing equality between the sexes, and a utopia demonstrating that "the cultural definitions of women's character were erroneous."[8] It is a book that satirizes nineteenth-century attitudes that limited women's sphere and fixed her "nature" as pious and pure. It also criticizes a commonly held nineteenth-century belief that women and men were quite different beings, illustrating through a series of "parallels" just how similar the two sexes are. At the same time, it also envisions a utopia where the values traditionally associated with women — unselfishness, nurture, and mutual support form the basis for the culture.

*Parallel* opens with a conventional utopian ploy: a first-person narrator lands his "aeroplane" on Mars, where he is introduced to the quite different perceptions and actions of Martian people through conversations with his guide, Severnius, and his guide's sister, Elodia. The nameless narrator is firmly rooted in his America of the 1890s and thus his amazement at the differences in people and mores provides the reading audience with a reference point, much the same way Van and his male colleagues would provide readers of Charlotte Perkins Gilman's *Herland* with that same kind of grounding some twenty-three years later.

But Alice and Ella's narrator is also a gullible innocent who is, to say the least, a bit slow on the uptake. Alice used a similar type of male narrator in a short story in the November 1882 *Lippincott's Monthly Magazine,* when she created the journalist Mark Bushman of "Mark Bushman's Romance." In this earlier story, the naïve narrator becomes the unwitting vehicle whereby a clever young woman obtains the man she loves. The narrator is blinded by his vision of this woman as passive and listless; all the time Mark is mooning over her "dainty poise," Eva is planning how she will make use of this silly man. As in the ironically titled "Mark Bushman's Romance," much of the humor of *Unveiling a Parallel* stems from the contrast between how the narrator expects women to act and how women, particularly the beautiful Elodia, do act when they are equal to men. No matter what evidence to the contrary looms before his eyes, the narrator tries rather desperately to stick to his preconceived notions about woman's sacred "nature."

Upon first landing on Mars, the narrator believes that he has found utopia. In the city of Thursia, where he is visiting, both sexes wear comfortable "womanish" white clothing, eat fruit and cereal but no meat, and love to contemplate beautiful art. Elodia and her brother listen to music, sit in couches made of down cushions, walk on lamb's wool rugs, and sleep in beds curtained in silk. The world the narrator enters is a splendid one, replete with sensuous pleasures associated with women of wealth and refinement.

In the midst of this elegance, the narrator looks and acts out of place. He continues to repeat remarkably stupid biases about Woman, telling Severnius that women in America are all "angels" who are treated "more as princesses than as inferiors" (29). Yet he has to admit that entire fields are closed to women; and, with prodding, he admits that many women do often have to support themselves and their children with menial jobs. He brags about American women not voting but reluctantly admits that women's property can be taxed. By contrast the world of Thursia — where women do vote, do hold public office, and do enter a profession because of their own inclinations—seems like utopia.

Elodia, particularly, appears to be a true utopian woman, as opposed to a True Woman, that venerated abstraction of nineteenth-century American mythology. Elodia, whose face is both intelligent and soft, walks in free, long steps and is both a banker and the president of the local school board. Yet, as the characters talk, we begin to realize that Elodia is not an ideal utopian woman; she has, in effect, adopted all the appropriate characteristics necessary for a "successful" male in America. First, we learn that Elodia drinks, often to excess. We hear that she is the "Supreme Sorceress" of a secret society, the Auroras who, during and after their women-only meetings, often drink too much champagne; Elodia, in fact, returns from a night with the Auroras quite hung over. Then, we learn that she "vaporizes," or uses the terrible-smelling valerian root mixed with alcohol, a habit that gives some momentary pleasure but can be fatal. Finally, we learn that Elodia, though unmarried, has a six-year-old daughter, with whom she does not live.

As the world of Thursia unfolds, we uncover a culture that is remarkably similar to that of the United States in the 1890s, but this world is an ironically egalitarian one where women can indulge their appetites as much as men. Besides seeing the effects of an Auroras' meeting on Elodia, the narrator also sees a game of "fisticuffs" and is horrified to discover the participants are women. He is flabbergasted when a car on a train is reserved for women where they can vaporize. But his final horror is discovering "Cupid's Gardens," an idyllic country garden and mansion with "chaste and beautiful statuary, the fountains, brooklets, arbors, and retreats" (75). Severnius explains that

Cupid's Gardens is the place that powerful, wealthy women meet their lovers or male prostitutes.

Despite obvious parallels with contemporary North American culture — the secret male societies, the "manly art" of prize-fighting, the "smoking" cars reserved for men, and widespread prostitution — the narrator is horrified because these vices are indulged in by women. Though Thursia is an egalitarian state where both men and women are equally permitted by custom and by law to indulge their lusts, what we *see* is a role reversal. The male guide, Severnius, is a rather pious astronomer who does not indulge in excess, although his sister does. His friend Massilia has a wife, Claris, who has "broken her husband's heart," because "women of her sort" find love to be an "ephemeral passion" (79).

Primarily, though, we see Elodia, whose "woman's nature" is neither better nor worse than man's. Although Elodia happens to be female, her gender in no way distracts us from the fact that she has stereotypical "male" desires. Elodia — like Kate Chopin's Edna Pontellier, whose hedonism would scandalize readers six years later — is concerned above all with her own pleasure. As Elodia says, "we are put into a material world, to enjoy material benefits" (74). Her life consists of all that money can buy — beautiful clothes, priceless art, soothing food, constant entertainment. She is in no way a passive "true" woman, who is content to serve others while sacrificing herself; Elodia is a sexual being who thinks of herself first and appears to enjoy life thoroughly.

One of the pleasures of *Parallel* is that Jones and Merchant do not condemn Elodia to an almost-certain death called for in sentimental literature. Indeed, they point out, through Elodia's dialogue, just how natural it is for her to want the power and pleasures afforded her as an adult member of a society that values materialistic things and sensuous pleasures. Elodia is allowed to win arguments, to be smarter than the narrator. With precise, irrefutable logic, Elodia demolishes her narrator's biases about women's "natures" in the United States where "men are strong, women are gentle, where women are faithful, men are brave" (107):

> "How charming to have the one nature dovetail into the other so neatly!" she exclaimed. "I seem to see a vision. . . . In the beginning . . . there was a heap of Qualities stacked in a pyramid upon the Earth. And the human creatures were requested to step up and help themselves to such as suited their tastes. There was a great scramble, and your sex, having some advantages in the way of muscle and limb, — and not having yet acquired the arts of courtesy and gallantry . . . pressed forward and took first choice. Naturally you selected the things which were agreeable to possess in themselves . . . such virtues as chastity, temperance, patience, modesty, piety, and some minor graces were thrust aside, and eventually forced upon the weaker sex." (107)

On this level, *Unveiling a Parallel* is an astute satire of the nineteenth-century mores that insisted upon women exhibiting only "agreeable," passive characteristics. To reinforce their satiric intent, the authors turn the traditional imagery associated with women and their purity inside out, constantly tricking the narrator and us. The Mars that the narrator enters is a very female one in its constant imagery of color and shape. The world is a "pink envelope," a "roseate color" (2). The narrator's first act upon landing is to pluck a cluster of ripe fruit and eat the rich berries growing on a beautiful tree. He then enters a white mansion, which, we soon find out, houses the beautiful Elodia. The sexual imagery of a male outsider, intruding upon the pink "envelope" that houses Elodia, is explicit. Yet Elodia, as we soon discover, is not a pink maiden whose head (real or metaphorical) is about to be penetrated by the narrator. Elodia is impenetrable, her logic irrefutable.

We are also given images that conjure up a particular expectation only to have that expectation deconstructed. When the narrator first hears of the society of the Auroras, he learns that the group originated several centuries ago in a time of great famine. The wealthiest women of the country banded together to relieve the suffering; their faces "beamed with such a light of salvation" that they soon were known as the auroras. Because they banished hunger so magically they were also called "sorcerers" (37). Elodia, as the "Supreme Sorceress," looks like a queen as she marches at the head of the parade that commemorates the good work of the Auroras. When the narrator and Severnius visit the Temple of the Auroras, they find a "lady" playing an instrument that resembles a harp. But all the images that ascribe selfless and angelic virtues to the women of Thursia are soon turned inside out. Elodia is anything but an angel. The "lady" playing the harp turns out to be Claris, the woman who has broken her faithful husband's heart. The Auroras are a group of women who carouse late into the night.

In addition, Jones and Merchant have great fun in using the color white to emphasize the lack of purity in Thursia. Though the sky is a gentle pink, all the details on the terrain in Thursia are white. Houses are white, clothes are soft and white or "cream-colored." The narrator sees white horses, alabaster skin (through which a pink light shines), white flowers, white sails, white clouds (in a pink sky), Elodia's white hand, and even white shoes. This overemphasis on the supposed color of purity in a city of rampant materialism provides a clear contrast to the second city on Mars that the narrator visits.

The authors, thus, do not end their book with just this satirical note: they offer us an alternative to the nineteenth-century dilemma — to be either a passive, chaste female or a greedy, lustful "male." The entire last quarter of their novel is a description of a second city on Mars, Lunismar, in the country of Caskia, where people have attained a more perfect state of development than in Thursia (or, by inference, in the United States). In Lunismar, our narrator finds that greed and "the lusts of the flesh" have disappeared (along with the constant repetition of the color white); in their place is egalitarianism based on honest labor and cheerful goodwill.

In the country of Caskia, we see happy children instead of white buildings full of priceless objets d'art. We hear that all races, ages, and classes are equal, that poverty does not exist. The Caskians, realizing that Mars is rich enough to maintain all its people in comfort, use technology for most of the heavy labor, thus allowing all people more leisure. The Caskian's use of new technology provides another contrast to Thursia (and America) where machinery increased the wealth of the rich. In Caskia, all share in the general good; all do meaningful work for the community. Underlying the country's social structure is a quasi-religious system of beliefs that emphasizes treating other people as one would like to be treated.

In Lunismar, our narrator finds another woman with whom to fall in love. The woman whom the narrator loves, Ariadne, is an heiress and a teacher in one of the city schools; in Caskia, family position does not keep one from wanting to serve humankind. In fact, the cook in Ariadne's home is also a leading scientist. Here, a mutual helpfulness has replaced selfishness, an emphasis on the doing of good has replaced materialistic possessions. No one has the power Elodia does; no one smokes valerian or has children without living with them because neither would be in the best interests of the town and its people. In the land of Caskia, traditional "female" virtues have replaced the "male" ones in Thursia.

### *Parallel* within the Context of Utopian Literature

Most people who are familiar with *Unveiling a Parallel* know of it as one of a group of books forming the late nineteenth-century American utopian tradition that followed in the wake of the publication of Edward Bellamy's popular *Looking Backward* (1888). Indeed, *Parallel* is one of over two hundred utopian novels published from 1888 through 1918 that envisions a better world—the largest single body of utopian writing in history.[9] The bulk of these books were written by unknown middle-aged, male writers, who were Protestant, middle class, and white. They promoted the virtues of a rural America while lambasting the evils of rampant capitalism. In these books, the spirit behind the Golden Rule could flourish; and thus the rhetoric often seemed more closely akin to a religious tract than an economic treatise. As Kenneth Roemer has written, "like the Social Gospel ministers of the 1880s and 1890s, the utopian authors not only painted the evils of the present in moralistic tones, they also envisioned the ultimate goals of the future in moralistic tones" (88), often using what David Bleich has called "a discourse of perfection."[10]

Like these other utopian novels, *Parallel* makes use of a familiar utopian plot formula whereby a visitor lands in a foreign world and is socialized through conversations with a guide and then prepares to return home. While in the strange, new world, this visitor sees how differently Martians (and how different Martians) live their lives and how their perceptions are parallel to and different from people living in the United States in the 1890s. The parallel between a corrupt Martian city and America and the contrast between an ideal Martian city and America implore readers to see their own world in the context of the narrative.

*Parallel,* like so many other utopian novels of its period, also incorporated the conventions of the familiar sentimental romance. In *Parallel,* a young unmarried man falls for one woman, is disillusioned, and then falls for a more appropriate woman. The contrast between the simple virtues of the "good" woman, and the worldly sinning of the "bad" woman appears to set up a familiar opposition. The story of the narrator's growing disillusionment provides the tension in the plot.

By writing within the framework of the utopian-sentimental tradition, Jones and Merchant were participating within their culture and helping familiarize their readers with a foreign world. Throughout the 1880s, Alice had been guiding readers' perceptions, heightening their morals, and helping them know how to behave through her sentimental romances and travel essays. In her novel and short stories, she had used, with great success, themes and structures familiar to her female readers: "good" women got rewarded, sometimes by marriage, other times by being the most moral character in the book; "bad" men did not recognize a worthy woman when they saw one and had to spend their lives alone or with a shrew.

In many important ways, though, *Parallel* is quite different from most utopian novels written during this time.[11] Unlike most utopian writers, Alice Ilgenfritz Jones and Ella Merchant were women and relatively young women at that. They saw, with far clearer eyes than the men, exactly what gender meant in nine-teenth-century America. Their imagery comes from women's bodies and lives; nowhere in *Parallel* does one volcano erupt — one of the most common images in the male utopian writers' canon, according to Kenneth Roemer. For Alice and Ella, as for many of the other women writing utopian literature during this period, the mere act of writing and publishing a novel that criticized their culture was a subversive act as well as an act of participation in the culture. Perhaps the very act of writing, par-ticularly writing a book critical of the mainstream culture's ideolo-gies and practices concerning women, encouraged women like Ella and Alice to envision utopia differently from the male writ-ers. Women's marginalized existence allowed them to see around (or through) the ideological blinders that made their culture's gender codes seem "natural" to the male authors. [12]

With few exceptions, the male utopian writers at the turn of the century accepted, with little questioning, their culture's gender ideology and reflected it in the content and structure of their novels. [13] Men imagined improved economic, religious, edu-cational, and political systems; but most retained their world's gender relationships and their concomitant cultural priorities. Though these male authors might well promote all kinds of "equal rights" for women, including a lack of financial dependence upon their husbands, they nevertheless defined women through their relation to their fathers, husbands, and children (Roemer 130).

Edward Bellamy's *Looking Backward*, the book many con-sider to be both the forerunner and the definer of a genre as it flowered in the late nineteenth century, illustrates how male au-thors reflected their culture's gender codes in the utopian litera-ture they wrote. In *Looking Backward*, protagonist Julian West wakes up in the year 2000 to a new egalitarian world full of technological advances. The new economic system, called "nationalism," is a thinly disguised socialism. Merchants and bankers have disappeared, as has money; everyone uses a credit card to charge purchases. Inheritance is not allowed; there is, in effect, no private property. All people have the same opportunity to higher education. Meals are served in central dining rooms or appear miraculously on a dumbwaiter in individual homes. Umbrellas cover the sidewalks automatically when it rains.

Yet, when we turn to family structure and women's roles within that family, we find a patriarchal family that is a remarkable replica of a late nineteenth-century Victorian family with "egalitarian" reform merely reinforcing the "father's" or "husband's" generosity. Julian West's guide in his new-found utopia, Dr. Leete, describes how the new system "permits" women to work because "it is fully understood that a certain regular requirement of labor, of a sort adapted to their powers, is well for body and mind." A woman is not "under [any] circumstances . . . permitted to follow any employment not perfectly adapted, both as to kind and degree of labor, to her sex" (210). One of the most important benefits of this "generous" male attitude, Leete tellingly reveals, is that women can now have "more power of giving happiness to men" (212).

*Looking Backward* ends with West about to marry his sweetheart, Edith Leete, a pure figment of a male fantasy. Edith spends her time shopping, blushing, and retiring early so that the men can talk meaningfully. As the epitome of the nineteenth-century True Woman, Edith's usefulness to the plot is illustrative: the very sense of her character helped familiarize nineteenth-century readers with a strange, socialist utopia. Having no will of her own, no "self," Edith exists to serve the male protagonist. Julian's marriage to her signifies *his* beginning in his brave, new world. Cultural practices decree that he will be better served as a married man — he will continue to quest while Edith will sooth his manners and raise his children, fluttering about taking care of his every psychic need. She will assure his personal utopia.

Like Bellamy, most other male utopian writers in the late nineteenth and early twentieth century glorified a patriarchy replete with the "male" priorities and privileges that replicated the culture in which they lived. Thus, while these writers proclaimed sexual equality to be an important goal in their utopian visions, their version of "equality" translated into a fictional utopia where men were served by utopian women, who looked and acted like submissive, passive "angels" in the house. Though women might be liberated economically, men still guided the state and created the policy, while women were assessed according to their relationships with men.

What makes *Parallel* particularly intriguing is that Jones and Merchant use the conventions available to them and at the same time manipulate them for their own purposes. What begins as a straight role reversal and satire ends as a utopian fantasy. Many earlier published role reversals within the utopian tradition were vehicles whereby authors could make fun of women's ambitions to be "like men," and they reinforced the "naturalness" of women's and men's "natures."[14] In British author Edward Bulwer-Lytton's 1871 *The Coming Race,* for example, the "new woman," who wears a different color to signify her sexual status, is satirized. Or, closer to home, Mrs. J. Wood's *Pantaletta, A Romance of Sheheland* (1882) satirizes a world where women rule and men spend their time gossiping, curling their hair, and wearing jewelry. General Gullible, the first-person journalist narrator, discovers an unmarked land in his "air-ship." He is subsequently captured and accused of being unlawfully clothed (wearing pants), for "upholding the obsolete distinctions between man and woman," and for wearing a beard in defiance of the law (41). The women, though they smoke and chew tobacco, often break into tears, yearning for the good old days. At the end of the narrative, General Gullible is about to marry the female president of the land. The women, says narrator Gullible, need to be relieved from political rights "in order that they may attend to greater and more complicated responsibilities" (136).

Similarly, Alice and Ella adopt certain elements from sentimental characterization but reject the kind of narrative endings Alice had used previously. The sentimental novel is, according to Jean Pfaelzer, a cultural fantasy through which social obligations were organized along segregated and idealized gender lines ("The Sentimental Promise," 86). Its authors often created pairs of characters that embodied opposing characteristics; most commonly authors created a "good" heroine who behaved according to prevailing gender codes and her foil, a "bad" woman, who did not. It often pitted these two kinds of women against each other, with the winner marrying and, if she had been particularly "good," perhaps having a male child. The sentimental novel affirmed the main character's true place in the world, and a happy ending meant finding that place. The place for the heroine was, inevitably, the private home, where she would remain. In Alice I. Jones's other works, her heroines inevitably married or became noble martyrs; the heroines' foils ended either miserable in an unhappy marriage or dead.

While recent feminist scholarship has pointed out that the sentimental novel was, indeed, all about women's power and moral authority,[15] the conventions associated with this genre nonetheless constricted women writers' prose into a masculinist shape. A sentimental romance had to "end" and had to end in a prescribed way, usually with the marriage of the heroine. This typical ending of a sentimental romance contradicted the heroine's power to control her own life. Marriage, as nineteenth-century women writers knew from the context of their own lives, ended some of a woman's power. The cultural practices that accompanied marriage in the late nineteenth century required women to relinquish autonomy in a myriad of small and large ways, such as giving up their names, subordinating their work to their husbands' career, or being responsible for housework and childcare to the exclusion of worldly activities.

Jones and Merchant subvert the masculinist hegemony of a "happy" ending first by not creating a heroine; instead they create a gullible, rather stupid male narrator who will search for an ideal relationship while learning about Martian customs. In the end, the male narrator readies himself to leave Mars, by himself. The women he has lusted after — Elodia in body and Ariadne in spirit — will both continue in their daily lives without him. Though Jones and Merchant appeared to have set up the women as foils, Ariadne, the woman who embodies all the elements of the cultural codes of "proper" behavior for late nineteenth-century women, does not end up with "her man" at the end of the book; nor does Elodia get punished for transgressing gender codes.

Jones and Merchant also subvert the sentimental structure by refusing to close their book with a prescribed ending. No one dies, no one marries. Life simply continues on. Their cleverness in ending their book is clearly illustrated when contrasted to other utopian-sentimental books written in the early 1890s by women. Many of the other women writers capitulated to the dictates of the "proper" ending of a novel, even if that ending undermined their main characters' power to control their own lives. For example, in *A New Aristocracy*, published in 1891, by "Birch Arnold," the *nom de plum* of Alice Elinor Bowen Bartlett,[16] the main character, Elsie Murchison, refuses a suitor midway through the book by saying "my hypersensitive soul has a right to its own distinct existence" (283). But by the end of the book, upon seeing this suitor frail and wan, Elsie capitulates and says: "The old wilful [*sic*], independent Elsie is dead, and I want to prove to you hereafter how patient and submissive I can be" (313). Elsie is last described vaguely as the "idol of her home . . . with children clinging to her skirts"; her distinct existence has vanished. The ending thus refutes the autonomy that Elsie has found, turning the utopian message inside out.

Similarly, the main characters in both of the novels of Helen Winslow, another Arena author, easily give up their meaningful work for marriage. In *Salome Shepherd* (also published in 1893), Salome, who has effected excellent Owenite reforms in her mills, marries in the last pages of the narrative. Despite her success, she says: "I shall leave the management of the mills to their new owner [her new husband]. It's no part of a married woman's business to manage her husband's office" (255). Her husband is pleased because he will have her "all to [him]self." Gertrude Van Deusen, the mayor in *A Woman for Mayor* (1909), tells her suitor, in fitting ways for a woman who has saved her town from financial doom and moral decay, why she cannot marry him:

> You would soon resent my attitude towards life; you would want to restrict my life, to surround me with invisible limitations, such as you believe all femininity should be hedged with. I couldn't endure it. I never had to, and I couldn't submit to being estimated every day and in the intimacy of home life — according to the old-fashioned standards that narrow a woman's heart and mind until they hold nothing but pettiness and

smallness and meanness of spirit. Because I couldn't, I should
make you the most unhappy of men. (322–23)

Yet, within a few pages Gertrude has decided not to run again
for mayor because it is not "appropriate" or "natural" for a woman
to run when there are acceptable male candidates. Her would-
be lover, of course, is elected. After he is almost killed, Gertrude
suddenly decides to marry him and the book ends "happily" because "the loving heart of the woman was to stand alongside the
strong desire of the man" (342). Both Salome and Gertrude leave
their successful lives as public reformers, remaking their communities in significant ways, for lives that are guaranteed to be
surrounded with all the invisible limitations that Gertrude astutely
predicted.

Other women writers within the utopian-sentimental tradition created "happy" endings only by eliminating their strong
"utopian" woman by the end of the book. In Mary Alice Tincker's *San Salvador* (1892), Iona, the smart central character, dies
protecting her utopia from three travelers who are about to discover it. She also dies because there is no place for her in utopia:
she has loved Dylar, the strong male character, who, in turn, loves
and marries the sweet, weak Tacita. Tacita, a woman who once
she became a mother "ceased to be anything else" (296), is the
woman who lives and gets her man and a male child as well.
The ideal woman is one, like Tacita, who will "rule the state
through the cradle" (302). The "good" woman has won the man
from the woman whose intelligence dooms her.[17] Similarly, in
Adela Orpen's *Perfection City* (1897), the founder of an intentional
community, Madame Morozoff-Smith, leaves her community in
the last chapter of the book "alone and unattended. No one knew
that she was going, and no one knew whither she went" (295).

Her departure allows Ezra and Olive Weston to be reunited, re-affirming their love and the importance of reforming the human heart before reforming the ways of the world (298).

Perhaps one reason Alice I. Jones and Ella Merchant escaped the pitfalls of the sentimental structure was that their ideal society was derived from one of the important subtexts of the sentimental romance — salvation through motherly love.[18] In the final third of their novel, they create a vision of what a world would be like if "motherly love" were, indeed, the dominant ideology in a culture. People take care of each other in Caskia; all, but particularly the very young and the very old, are nurtured. Gone is money-making for its own sake; gone also is gambling, drinking, smoking, and prostitution. Perhaps by providing this vision of a "good" life, a life without conflict and tension, Jones and Merchant were also able to escape from having to have a resolution, an ending, closure. Just as the process of mothering is an ever-ongoing one — children never "get raised"; one never has a finished "product" — so, by ending with a glimpse of Caskia, the authors relieve themselves of the necessity of tying all the ends of a "story" together. The narrator may be leaving, but the emphasis is no longer on him; rather, it is on the world of Caskia where the process of life will continue.

### A Personal Context

The material conditions and cultural practices that gave rise to my delight in discovering *Unveiling a Parallel* and my subsequent desire to share it are numerous. I was first introduced to popular utopian fiction of late nineteenth-century America by reading Edward Bellamy's *Looking Backward* in graduate school in the early 1970s. I remember quite clearly the day we discussed

the book: it was overly warm in the classroom, which was popu-
lated mostly with large, eager young men. As the class talked
about the institutions that Bellamy had altered, I felt a familiar
distancing from the direction the discussion was taking. I had
found the book offensive; the main female character, Edith Leete,
was, in my opinion, a simpering idiot. Any woman who spent
all her time blushing and retiring early so that the men could
talk was not worth wasting my reading time on.

I had little time to waste that year, having resigned from my
high school teaching job a few months earlier to pursue a Ph.D.
As a full-time student, teacher of freshman composition, and
single parent, I could not be bothered with women, real or fictional, who spent their time shopping. When I said as much in
class, I was told I was misreading the story. It was not a book
about *Edith;* she occupied fictional space to befriend and serve
the hero. When I said that was my point, exactly, the men stared
at me with a vacant, "that's why we don't want to admit women
to graduate schools" stare. "I want a utopia for me," I shouted
to them.

Disappointed that so-called utopian writers like Bellamy and
William Dean Howells in his *Traveler from Altruria* (1894) and its
sequel, *Through the Eye of the Needle* (1907), did not alter conventional and depressingly stultifying nineteenth-century expectations about gender, I turned to women writers for an insight
into utopia that the male authors missed. When I finally read
*Parallel,* I was instantly delighted with the satire and with the open-
endedness of the narrative. As a contemporary reader sick to
death of nineteenth-century novels in which lusty dark-haired
women are killed off at the end of the book and where the blue-
eyed blonde gets her man, I am a real sucker for a dumb male
main character who is constantly outwitted by a smart woman;

I am equally pleased when I find a female character in nineteenth-century literature who admits to sins of the flesh. To foreground my biases here — I am fascinated by a book that questions woman's "proper" sphere and role in the late nineteenth-century America at a time when other books, especially "utopian" books, were markedly silent on the subject. I could love *Parallel* if only for the fact that Elodia does not die at the end.

*Parallel* is important to me because of the questions it raises and the issues it anticipates. Susan Harris has written that one way to evaluate sentimental fiction by nineteenth-century women is to ask what later ideological or political debate it anticipates and what textual trace-markers could have helped change the shape of later women's novels.[19] Alice I. Jones and Ella Merchant anticipate by twenty-three years the concerns that Charlotte Perkins Gilman was to raise in *Herland.* Like *Herland, Unveiling a Parallel* is narrated by a man, who begins his journey to understanding by disbelieving what he sees. Like *Herland, Parallel* explodes an essentialist definition of woman's "nature" and imagines a world where the values associated with motherhood have the highest priority. But unlike Gilman, Jones and Merchant use narrative strategies that allow them to alter the dominant sentimental conventions or, in the words of Rachel Blau Du-Plessis, to "write beyond the ending."[20]

Although the land of Herland is woman-centered, the shape of the narrative is not. Gilman's utopian *Herland* includes, in one of its narrative highlights, a marriage of the three men who are visitors in Herland with the three young Herland women, thus "affirming" the women by conventional standards, despite the fact that the sexual instinct has been bred out of the Herland women over centuries without men and that the very existence of these three men threatens the welfare of the community. Similarly,

Gilman ends her earlier utopian novel *Moving the Mountain* (1908) with an equally stereotypical marriage of the male narrator with a country woman. The marriage, Gilman implies, will "save" the woman because she will now be able to move to a city where she can join in cooperative efforts with other women. Nonetheless, the act of marrying must precede liberation. Likewise, Gilman's sequel to *Herland, With Her in Ourland,* ends with the birth of Van and Ellador's male child. To their credit, Jones and Merchant refuse to play by the sentimental rules; and their book, thus, both anticipates Gilman and allows them to escape Gilman's reliance upon conventional sentimental endings that valorize heterosexual love and affirm the necessity of a resolution of conflict.

What also fascinates me is the fact that Alice Ilgenfritz Jones and Ella Merchant were Cedar Rapids matrons. They did not descend from the Beecher line, as Gilman did, or have friends and relatives involved in a variety of radical causes. Where did their spark come from? What allowed them to say the things they did? Did their insight come from the unknown ingredient here — Ella Merchant? Alice had been a professional writer, but her writing both before and after *Parallel* never strayed far from the bounds of convention. Her women characters had spunk, perhaps, and may have outwitted the less smart male narrators, but they inevitably ended up married or dead or working as missionaries. Alice alone never wrote beyond the ending. But together with Ella, something happened; and the two authors leave us with a book that critiques their world in ways few of the male writers did, while positing a new, utopian land for women.

As a modern reader, my one problem with the book is my resistance to the utopian land of Caskia laid out for me. Like so many other twentieth-century readers, I prefer the lustful

Elodia to the sweet Ariadne. I am put off by the vaguely religious, abstract language — the language of spiritualist fiction —
that takes over in Caskia; I dislike the idea that a male "Master"
gently instructs the narrator in the quiet and efficient ways of
Caskians. I question why utopia must be linked with traditional
Christian values and why sexual passion must always be eliminated. I enjoy the book more when it satirizes; when it shifts
to a fixed utopian land, my notion that anything is possible is
narrowed down to one vision, limited by its linguistic and cultural contexts.

The Caskian version of utopia, with its sexlessness and pious
women, has caused my contemporaries problems as well. Barbara Quissell simply dismisses the entire Caskian chapters as "the
last laugh." Kenneth Roemer, more in line with my beliefs here,
writes that this last part of *Parallel* is Jones and Merchant's nego-
tiation between their implied attitudes and expected responses
by nineteenth-century readers. Having deconstructed a series of
notions about sex roles, he says, they tried to reconstruct a view
of gender to fill in the vacuum. They filled this void by using
what were familiar and meaningful means of reconstruction —
Christian views, nationalism, and sentimentality. [21]

What we all have to remember, though, is that few of us living in this final decade of the twentieth century can fully appreciate the impulse behind Alice and Ella's (and Charlotte's) desire
to get rid of male lusts. Having access to birth control, to our
own money, to our children in cases of divorce, we are no longer
as dependent in our private lives on the goodness of men. Should
our husbands be alcoholics or gamblers, our own destinies are
not irrevocably doomed as well. Women such as Alice I. Jones
and Ella Merchant, living just as the twentieth century began
and imbued with the language of the Social Gospel movement

and Christian spirituality, negotiated the path to a better world for women the best they could.

This past year, almost twenty years later, I taught Bellamy's *Looking Backward* in my American Novel class at Hood College, a women's college. As soon as class began my students wanted to talk about Edith. "What a wimp," they told me; "what a useless tool of the patriarchy." Toward the end of the period, I read the students excerpts from *Unveiling a Parallel*. After I finished a rather lengthy reading, the students responded with pleasure. To them, the mere fact that a dumb man's dumb ideas about women were being made fun of made the book an instant success. They were also not nearly as put off by what strikes me as a boring Caskian utopia. "Look," they told me, "at least women really are equal to men. Old people are being taken care of, children are loved, and no one is being oppressed." "How can you," they said, "not like a place where good food is taken seriously." And to that, I cannot reply. *Unveiling a Parallel* has something to offer all of us.

### Notes

1. See the excerpts of reviews in Benjamin Flower's monthly magazine, *The Arena*, for November 1896; the June 30, 1893, *Cedar Rapids Evening Gazette;* and the review (no author no date) pasted inside a copy of the first edition of *Parallel* in the Frederick Lewis Pattee Library of the Pennsylvania State University.

2. See, for example, E. A. Alderman and Joel Chandler Harris, *Library of Southern Literature*, vol. 15, (Atlanta: Martin & Hoyt Co., 1909), 228, which lists Alice I. Jones, the author of *The Chevalier de St. Denis,* as a Louisiana writer. This error has been compounded by more current bibliographers including Lizzie Carter McVoy and Ruth Bates Campbell in their *Bibliography of Fiction by Louisianians and on Louisiana Subjects* (Baton Rouge: Louisiana Univ. Press,

1935), in which they label Jones as a "Louisiana Author." Most recently, Susan
Miller Williams includes a discussion of Jones's novel *Beatrice of Bayou Teche*
in "Love and Rebellion: Louisiana Women Novelists, 1865–1919" (Ph.D. diss.,
Louisiana State Univ., 1984).

3. Jones and Merchant obliquely refer to the Social Hygiene movement
on pages 77–78 of their text. The movement dealt with, among other things,
sexual behavior relative to individual and social aspects of health. Its advo-
cates promoted chastity and male self-control, while trying to correct social
ills resulting in problems such as prostitution and venereal disease.

4. Scant material on the lives of either Ella Merchant or Alice Ilgenfritz
Jones exists today. My information comes from their obituaries, their cemetery listings, city directories, their local newspaper, *The Cedar Rapids Gazette*,
and a variety of authorless local histories such as *The Portrait and Biographical
Album of Linn County, Iowa* (Chicago: Chapman Brothers, 1887) and *The History
of Butler and Bremer Counties, Iowa* (Springfield, Ill.: Union Publishing Co., 1883).

5. For this review of *Beatrice*, see the *Bookman* (Jan. 1896): 433. See also
Susan Miller William's dissertation, "Love and Rebellion," 139–45, for a discussion of *Beatrice*.

6. For a review of *The Chevalier*, see the *New York Times*, December 15, 1900.

7. See the *Cedar Rapids Gazette*, Monday, March 5, 1906, and Thursday,
March 8, 1906. Young Isabelle, after graduating from high school, went to the
Art Institute in Chicago for five years and graduated from the Department
of Painting and Drawing. In the words of the *Cedar Rapids Gazette*, Isabelle had
"a talent for both painting and drawing" and had worked as an illustrator. She
married a childhood sweetheart, Herbert Fleming, in May 1907. Like Isabelle's
stepmother, Herbert was a writer, working both as a newspaper reporter and
as a free-lance author for magazines.

8. Carol Farley Kessler has called *Parallel* "almost" a "gender role reversal," in *Daring to Dream: Utopian Fiction by United States Women, 1836–1919* (Boston:
Routledge, Pandora Press, 1984). She adds that the central parallel unveiled
is that the sexes are more similar than different. Kessler's excerpts from *Parallel* —
pages 40–58, 158–78, and 182–87 — in *Daring to Dream* mark its first reproduction
since its Arena publication. Also writing about *Parallel* are Lyman Tower Sargent,
who calls it a utopia stressing equality between the sexes, and Barbara Quissell,
who writes that the cultural definitions of women's character are erroneous.
See also Stuart Teitler's introduction to Mary Bradley Lane's *Mizora* (1881; re-

print, Boston: Gregg Press, 1978), where he discusses *Parallel* within the context of feminist fantasy.

9. The statistics that follow are summarized from Kenneth Roemer's excellent book *The Obsolete Necessity: America in Utopian Writings, 1888-1900* (Kent, Ohio: Kent State Univ. Press, 1976). See also Roemer's *America as Utopia: Collected Essays* (New York: B. Franklin, 1980). Others who have written about this same explosion of utopian literature include Jean Pfaelzer, *The Utopian Novel in America, 1886-1896: The Politics of Form* (Pittsburgh, Pa.: Univ. of Pittsburgh Press, 1984) and Peter Ruppert, *Reader in a Strange Land: The Activity of Reading Literary Utopias* (Athens, Ga.: Univ. of Georgia Press, 1986).

10. Bleich defines "discourse of perfection" as writing that "justifies war in the name of a higher morality or articulates the hope for social justice with the vocabulary of religious salvation or both" ("Sexism and the Discourse of Perfection," *American Transcendental Quarterly* 3 [Mar. 1989]: 13). Bleich is more cynical than Roemer in his assessment as to who was writing utopian novels. Utopian literature, he says, is a "genre invented and sustained by men who wanted power, didn't get it, and wrote books about the best of all possible worlds to create a vicarious kingship for themselves" (12).

11. For discussions of late nineteenth-century utopian writing by women, see Carol Kessler's excellent introduction to *Daring to Dream* and my essay "Women Seeing Utopia: Patterns in Utopian Literature, 1880-1915," in *Utopie per Gli Anni Ottanta* (Rome, Italy: Gangemi Editore, 1986), 499-511. See also chapter 7 of Jean Pfaelzer's *Utopian Novel in America;* Daphne Patai's "Utopia for Whom?" *Aphra* 5 (Summer 1974): 2-16; Lyman Tower Sargent's "Women in Utopia," *Comparative Literature Studies* 10 (Dec. 1973): 302-15; Nan B. Albinski's "Utopia Reconsidered: Women Novelists and Nineteenth-Century Utopian Visions," *Signs* 13 (1988): 830-41; chapter 1 of Frances Bartkowski's *Feminist Utopias* (Lincoln: Univ. of Nebraska Press, 1989); and Libby Falk Jones and Sarah Webster Goodwin's edited volume, *Feminism, Utopia, and Narrative* (Knoxville: Univ. of Tennessee Press, 1990).

12. It is interesting to note that this book was not (could not be?) published by one of Alice I. Jones's mainstream publishers — Lippincott or McClurg. Jones and Merchant probably had to pay for *Parallel*'s printing. See Roger Stoddard, "Vanity and Reform: B. O. Flower's Arena Publishing Company, Boston, 1890-1896," *Papers on the Bibliographic Society of America* 76 (1982): 273-334. Stoddard's essay includes a standard Arena contract.

13. A few of the male writers also questioned their culture's prevailing gender ideology in the pages of their utopian novels. The most obvious example is Alcanoan O. Grigsby, whose 1900 novel, *Nequa,* describes a world where both sexes are equal after women put an end to war and demanded freedom from the domination of man-made laws. "Mother-love" dominates the new world. Perhaps it is the subject matter that has confused critics such as Barbara Quissell into thinking that Grigsby was female. See Quissell's "New World That Eve Made: Feminist Utopias Written by Nineteenth-Century Women," in Roemer's *America as Utopia,* where she discusses Grigsby as a woman writer. Another male writer who attacked gender distinctions was Henry Olerich in *A Cityless and Countryless World* (1893), a story of a Martian visiting America. See also the utopias of Linn Boyd Porter *(Speaking of Ellen,* 1890) and John McCoy *(A Prophetic Romance,* 1896), in which women have leadership roles. Although Edward Bellamy's most famous utopia, *Looking Backward,* does not fit into this category, his 1897 sequel, *Equality,* would fit here. In *Equality,* women work in all professions and the simpering, non-working Edith Leete of *Looking Backward* is a farm hand in the sequel.

14. At least one other role reversal also satirized gender expectations; see Annie Denton Cridge's *Man's Rights; or, How Would You Like It,* published in 1870. Carol Farley Kessler has reprinted the first part of the book in *Daring to Dream,* 74–94. Cridge and her husband, Alfred, were reformers in the 1860s in Washington, D.C., advocating, among other things, co-operative kitchens and workshops, education based on "natural" principles, and publication of tracts "to free the masses from Orthodox control." See Cridge's letter on "The Society of Co-Workers" in the *Boston Investigator,* April 1, 1868.

See also Stuart Teitler's introduction to *Mizora,* where he discusses works of feminist fantasy that deal with role reversals; and see Daphne Patai's "When Women Rule: Defamiliarization and the Sex-Role Reversal Utopia," *Extrapolation* 23 (Spring 1982): 56–69.

15. Recent critics such as Jane Tompkins have shown us that, in Tompkins' words, "out of the ideological materials they had at their disposal, the sentimental novelists elaborated a myth that gave women the central position of power and authority in the culture" (83). Tompkins argues that salvation through motherly love gives women this central position of authority. See "Sentimental Power: *Uncle Tom's Cabin* and the Politics of Literary History," in *The New Feminist Criticism: Essays on Women, Literature, Theory,* ed. Elaine Showalter

(New York: Random, Pantheon Books, 1985), 81–105. See also Dee Garrison's essay "Immoral Fiction in the Late Victorian Library," *American Quarterly* 28 (Spring 1976): 71–80, where she argues that sentimental fiction subverts traditional male authority.

16. See Carol Farley Kessler's annotated bibliographical commentary on "Birch Arnold" in *Daring to Dream*, 241.

17. Perhaps this unquestioning sentimental ending is one reason that Mary Alice Tincker remained a popular writer for *Lippincott's Monthly Magazine*, while Alice I. Jones did not.

18. Just as Jones and Merchant were creators when it came to constructing an ending for their book, they used the material at hand to give their vision shape. Their perfect world stemmed from a variety of movements and writings with which they must have been familiar. Both the Social Gospel movement—with its emphasis on pious women doing the work of the church—and the Social Hygiene movement—with its emphasis on chastity—contributed to their vision. Similarly, their vision stemmed from the traces left by writers such as Harriet Beecher Stowe, who in *Uncle Tom's Cabin* offers Rachel's woman-centered kitchen as a utopian alternative to a materialistic slave state. Or their vision might have come from such writers as Louisa May Alcott, who in *Work* surrounds her heroine with a loving circle of women whose antimaterialistic values of sisterhood continue to encourage countless generations of women. Or, perhaps, their vision began with Mary Bradley Lane's utopian novel, *Mizora,* published first in 1881 and then reprinted in 1889, in which a visitor to a women's utopia dies because she cannot translate the values she has discovered in the center of the earth into the cold, materialistic, heterosexual world she reenters.

19. See Harris's essay "But is it any *good?*: Notes Toward an Evaluative Methodology for Nineteenth-Century American Women's Fiction," *American Literature* 63 (Mar. 1991): 43–61.

20. DuPlessis writes that these tactics of writing beyond the ending might result in woman-to-woman bonds. She finds the romance plot muffles the main character by repressing quest, by valorizing heterosexual ties, and by offering coupling as a sign of personal and narrative success.

21. See Barbara Quissell's essay "The New World That Eve Made," 157; Kenneth Roemer's comments come from an unpublished letter, July 25, 1990.

## Works Cited

Albinski, Nan Bowman. "Utopia Reconsidered: Women Novelists and Nineteenth-Century Utopian Visions." *Signs* 13 (1988): 830–41.

Alderman, E. A., and Joel Chandler Harris, eds. *Library of Southern Literature,* vol. 15. Atlanta: Martin & Hoyt Co., 1909.

Arnold, Birch, [Bartlett, Alice E.]. *A New Aristocracy.* New York: 1891.

Bartkowski, Frances. *Feminist Utopias.* Lincoln: Univ. of Nebraska Press, 1989.

Bellamy, Edward. *Looking Backward.* 1887. Reprint. New York: Modern Library, 1951.

Bleich, David. "Sexism and the Discourse of Perfection." *American Transcendental Quarterly* 3 (Mar. 1989): 11–27.

Bleiler, Everett F. *Science-Fiction: The Early Years.* Kent, Ohio: Kent State Univ. Press, 1990.

*Cedar Rapids Gazette,* June 30, 1893; March 5, 1906; March 8, 1906; May 1, 1907.

Cridge, Annie Denton. "The Society of Co-Workers." *The Boston Investigator,* April 1, 1868.

DuPlessis, Rachel Blau. *Writing Beyond the Ending.* Bloomington: Indiana Univ. Press, 1985.

Garrison, Dee. "Immoral Fiction in the Late Victorian Library." *American Quarterly* 28 (Spring 1976): 71–80.

Gilman, Charlotte Perkins. *Herland.* 1915. Reprint. New York: Random, Pantheon Books, 1979.

Harris, Susan. "'But is it any *good?:* Notes Toward an Evaluative Methodology for Nineteenth-Century American Women's Fiction." *American Literature* 63 (Mar. 1991): 43–61.

*History of Butler and Bremer Counties, Iowa, The.* Springfield, Ill.: Union Publishing Co., 1883.

Jones, Alice Ilgenfritz. *Beatrice of Bayou Teche.* Chicago: A. C. McClurg & Co., 1895.

————. *The Chevalier of St. Denis*. Chicago: A. C. McClurg & Co., 1900.

————. "Down the Red River." *Lippincott's Monthly Magazine* (Feb. 1881): 113–23.

————. [Ferris Jerome, pseud.]. *High-Water-Mark*. Philadelphia: J. B. Lippincott & Co., 1879.

————. "The Lakes of Minnesota." *Lippincott's Monthly Magazine* (Mar. 1880): 265–75.

————. "Mark Bushman's Romance." *Lippincott's Monthly Magazine* (Nov. 1882): 497–506.

————. "Westbrook." *Lippincott's Monthly Magazine* (Aug. 1880): 218–32.

Jones, Libby Falk, and Sarah Webster Goodwin, eds. *Feminism, Utopia, and Narrative*. Knoxville: Univ. of Tennessee Press, 1990.

Kessler, Carol Farley, ed. *Daring to Dream: Utopian Stories by United States Women, 1836–1919*. Boston: Routledge, Pandora Press, 1984.

Kolmerten, Carol. "Women Seeing Utopia: Patterns in Utopian Literature, 1880–1915." In *Utopie per Gli Anni Ottanta*, ed. Guiseppa Saccaroo del Buffa and Arthur O. Lewis. Rome, Italy: Gangemi Editore, 1986, 499–511.

Lane, Mary Bradley. *Mizora: A Prophecy*. 1881. Reprint. Boston: Gregg Press, 1978.

McVoy, Lizzie Carter, and Ruth Bates Campbell, eds. *Bibliography of Fiction by Louisianians and on Louisiana Subjects*. Baton Rouge: Louisiana Univ. Press, 1935.

Patai, Daphne. "Utopia for Whom?" *Aphra* 5 (Summer 1974): 2–16.

————. "When Women Rule: Defamiliarization in the Sex-Role Reversal Utopia." *Extrapolation* 23 (Spring 1982): 56–69.

Pfaelzer, Jean. "The Sentimental Promise and the Utopian Myth: Rebecca Harding Davis's "The Harmonists" and Louisa May Alcott's "Transcendental Wild Oats." *ATQ* 3 (Mar. 1989): 85–101.

————. *The Utopian Novel in America, 1886–1896*. Pittsburgh, Pa.: Univ. of Pittsburgh Press, 1984.

*Portrait and Biographical Album of Linn County, Iowa*. Chicago: Chapman Brothers, 1887.

Quissell, Barbara. "The New World That Eve Made: Feminist Utopias Written by Nineteenth-Century Women." In *American as Utopia*, ed. Kenneth Roemer. New York: B. Franklin, 1980, 148–74.

Roemer, Kenneth. *The Obsolete Necessity: America in Utopian Writings, 1888–1900.* Kent, Ohio: Kent State Univ. Press, 1976.

Roemer, Kenneth, ed. *America as Utopia: Collected Essays.* New York: B. Franklin, 1980.

Ruppert, Peter. *Reader in a Strange Land: The Activity of Reading Literary Utopias.* Athens, Ga.: Univ. of Georgia Press, 1986.

Sargent, Lyman Tower. "Women in Utopia." *Comparative Literature Studies* 10 (Dec. 1973): 302–15.

Stoddard, Roger. "Vanity and Reform: B. O. Flower's Arena Publishing Company, Boston, 1890–1896." *Papers of the Bibliographic Society of America* 76 (1982): 273–337.

Teitler, Stuart, ed., with Kristine Anderson. *Mizora: A Prophecy*, by Mary Bradley Lane, 1881, reprint. Boston: Gregg Press, 1975.

Tincker, Mary Agnes. *San Salvador.* 1892. Reprint. New York: Arno Press, 1978.

Tompkins, Jane. "Sentimental Power: *Uncle Tom's Cabin* and the Politics of Literary History." In *The New Feminist Criticism: Essays on Women, Literature, Theory*, ed. Elaine Showalter (New York: Random, Pantheon Books, 1985), 81–105.

Williams, Susan Miller. "Love and Rebellion: Louisiana Women Novelists, 1865–1919." Ph.D. diss. Louisiana State Univ., 1984.

Winslow, Helen. *Salome Shephard.* Boston: Arena Publishing Co., 1893.

———. *A Woman for Mayor.* Boston: Arena Publishing Co., 1909.

Wood, Mrs. J. *Pantaletta: A Romance of Sheheland.* New York: American News Co., 1882.

UNVEILING A PARALLEL

# CHAPTER 1.

A REMARKABLE ACQUAINTANCE.

"A new person is to me always a great event, and hinders me from sleep." — EMERSON.

You know how certain kinds of music will beat everything out of your consciousness except a wild delirium of joy; how love of a woman will take up every cranny of space in your being, — and fill the universe beside, — so that people who are not en rapport with the strains that delight you, or with the beauty that enthralls you, seem pitiable creatures, not in touch with the Divine Harmony, with Supreme Loveliness.

So it was with me, when I set my feet on Mars! My soul leaped to its highest altitude and I had but one vast thought, — "I have triumphed; I am here! And I am alone; Earth is unconscious of the glory that is mine!"

I shall not weary you with an account of my voyage, since you are more interested in the story of my sojourn on the red planet than in the manner of my getting there.

It is not literally red, by the way; that which makes it appear so at this distance is its atmosphere, — its "sky," — which is of a soft roseate color, instead of being blue like ours. It is as beautiful as a blush.

I will just say, that the time consumed in making the journey was incredibly brief. Having launched my aeroplane on the current of attraction which flows uninterruptedly between this world and that, traveling was as swift as thought. My impression is that my speed was constantly accelerated until I neared my journey's end, when the planet's pink envelope interposed its soft resistance to prevent a destructive landing.

I settled down as gently as a dove alights, and the sensation was the most ecstatic I have ever experienced.

When I could distinguish trees, flowers, green fields, streams of water, and people moving about in the streets of a beautiful city, it was as if some hitherto unsuspected chambers of my soul were flung open to let in new tides of feeling.

My coming had been discovered. A college of astronomers in an observatory which stands on an elevation just outside the city, had their great telescope directed toward the Earth, — just as our telescopes were directed to Mars at that time, — and they saw me and made me out when I was yet a great way off.

They were able to determine the exact spot whereon I would land, about a mile distant from the observatory, and repaired thither with all possible speed, — and they have very perfect means of locomotion, superior even to our electrical contrivances.

Before I had time to look about me, I found myself surrounded, and unmistakably friendly hands outheld to welcome me.

There were eight or ten of the astronomers, — some young, some middle-aged, and one or two elderly men. All of them, including the youngest, who had not even the dawn of a beard upon his chin, and the oldest, whose hair was silky white, were strikingly handsome. Their features were extraordinarily mobile and expressive. I never saw a more lively interest manifest on mortal countenances than appeared on theirs, as they bent their glances upon me. But their curiosity was tempered by a dignified courtesy and self-respect.

They spoke, but of course I could not understand their words, though it was easy enough to interpret the tones of their voices, their manner, and their graceful gestures. I set them down for a people who had attained to a high state of culture and good-breeding.

I suddenly felt myself growing faint, for, although I had not fasted long, a journey such as I had just accomplished is exhausting.

Near by stood a beautiful tree on which there was ripe fruit. Someone instantly interpreted the glance I involuntarily directed to it, and plucked a cluster of the large rich berries and gave them to me, first putting one in his own mouth to show me that it was a safe experiment.

While I ate, — I found the fruit exceedingly refreshing, — the company conferred together, and presently one of the younger men approached and took me gently by the arm and walked me away toward the city. The others followed us.

We had not to go farther than the first suburb. My companion, whom they called Severnius, turned into a beautiful park, or grove, in the midst of which stood a superb mansion built of dazzling white stone. His friends waved us farewells with their hands, — we responding in like manner, — and proceeded on down the street.

I learned afterwards that the park was laid out with scientific precision. But the design was intricate, and required study to follow the curves and angles. It seemed to me then like an exquisite mood of nature.

The trees were of rare and beautiful varieties, and the shrubbery of the choicest. The flowers, whose colors could not declare themselves, — it being night, — fulfilled their other delightful function and tinctured the balmy air with sweet odors.

Paths were threaded like white ribbons through the thick greensward.

As we walked toward the mansion, I stopped suddenly to listen to a most musical and familiar and welcome sound, — the splash of water. My companion divined my thought. We turned aside, and a few steps brought us to a marble fountain. It was in the form of a chaste and lovely female figure, from whose chiseled fingers a shower of glittering drops continually poured. Severnius took an alabaster cup from the base of the statue, filled it, and offered me a drink. The water was sparkling and intensely cold, and had the suggestion rather than the fact of sweetness.

"Delicious!" I exclaimed. He understood me, for he smiled and nodded his head, a gesture which seemed to say, "It gives me pleasure to know that you find it good." I could not conceive of his expressing himself in any other than the politest manner.

We proceeded into the house. How shall I describe that house? Imagine a place which responds fully to every need of the highest culture and taste, without burdening the senses with oppressive luxury, and you have it! In a word, it was an ideal house and home. Both outside and inside, white predominated. But here and there were bits of color the most brilliant, like jewels. I found that I had never understood the law of contrast, or of economy in art; I knew nothing of "values," or of relationships in this wonderful realm, of which it may be truly said, "Fools rush in where angels fear to tread."

I learned subsequently that all Marsians of taste are sparing of rich colors, as we are of gems, though certain classes indulge in extravagant and gaudy displays, recognizing no law but that which permits them to have and to do whatsoever they like.

I immediately discovered that two leading ideas were carried out in this house; massiveness and delicacy. There was extreme solidity in everything which had a right to be solid and stable; as the walls, and the supporting pillars, the staircases, the polished floors, and some pieces of stationary furniture, and the statuary, — the latter not too abundant. Each piece of statuary, by the way, had some special reason for being where it was; either it served some practical purpose, or it helped to carry out a poetical idea, — so that one was never taken aback as by an incongruity.

Some of the floors were of marble, in exquisite mosaic-work, and others were of wood richly inlaid. The carpets were beautiful, but they were used sparingly. When we sat down in a room a servant usually brought a rug or a cushion for our feet. And when we went out under the trees they spread carpets on the grass and put pillows on the rustic seats.

The decorations inside the house were the most airy and graceful imaginable. The frescoes were like clouds penetrated by the rarest tints, — colors idealized, — cunningly wrought into surpassingly lovely pictures, which did not at once declare the artist's intention, but had to be studied. They were not only an indulgence to the eye, but a charming occupation for the thoughts. In fact, almost everything about the place appealed to the higher faculties as well as to the senses.

There comes to us, from time to time, a feeling of disenchantment toward almost everything life has to offer us. It never came to me with respect to Severnius' house. It had for me an interest and a fascination which I was never able to dissect, any more than you would be able to dissect the charm of the woman you love.

With all its fine artistic elaborations, there was a simplicity about it which made it possible for the smallest nature to measure its capacity there, as well as the greatest. The proper sort of a yardstick for all uses has inch-marks.

Severnius took me upstairs and placed a suite of rooms at my command, and indicated to me that he supposed I needed rest, which I did sorely. But I could not lie down until I had explored my territory.

The room into which I had been ushered, and where Severnius left me, closing the noiseless door behind him, looked to me like a pretty woman's boudoir, — almost everything in it being of a light and delicate color. The walls were cream-tinted, with a deep frieze of a little darker shade, relieved by pale green and brown decorations. The wood work was done in white enamel paint. The ceiling was sprinkled with silver stars. Two or three exquisite water-colors were framed in silver, and the andirons, tongs and shovel, and the fender round the fire-place, and even the bedstead, were silver-plated.

The bed, which stood in an alcove, was curtained with silk, and had delicacies of lace also, as fine and subtle as Arachne's web. The table and a few of the chairs looked like our spindle-legged Chippendale things. And two or three large rugs might have been of Persian lamb's wool. A luxurious couch was placed across one corner of the room and piled with down cushions. An immense easy chair, or lounging chair, stood opposite.

The dressing table, of a peculiarly beautiful cream-colored wood, was prettily littered with toilet articles in carved ivory or silver mountings. Above it hung a large mirror. There was a set of shelves for books and bric-a-brac; a porphyry lamp-stand with a lamp dressed in an exquisite pale-green shade; a chiffonier of marquetry.

The mantel ornaments were vases of fine pottery and marble statuettes. A musical instrument lay on a low bamboo stand. I could not play upon it, but the strings responded sweetly to the touch.

A little investigation revealed a luxurious bath-room. I felt the need of a bath, and turned on the water and plunged in. As I finished, a clock somewhere chimed the hour of midnight.

Before lying down, I put by the window draperies and looked out. I was amazed at the extreme splendor of the familiar constellations. Owing to the peculiarity of the atmosphere of Mars, the night there is almost as luminous as our day. Every star stood out, not a mere twinkling eye, or little flat, silver disk, but a magnificent sphere, effulgent and supremely glorious.

Notwithstanding that it was long before I slept, I awoke with the day. I think its peculiar light had something to do with my waking. I did not suppose such light was possible out of heaven! It did not dazzle me, however; it simply filled me, and gave me a sensation of peculiar buoyancy.

I had a singular feeling when I first stepped out of bed, — that the floor was not going to hold me. It was as if I should presently be lifted up, as a feather is lifted by a slight current of air skimming along on the ground. But I soon found that this was not going to happen. My feet clung securely to the polished wood and the soft wool of the rug at the bedside. I laughed quietly to myself. In fact I was in the humor to laugh. I felt so happy. Happiness seemed to be a quality of the air, which at that hour was particularly charming in its freshness and its pinkish tones.

I had made my ablutions and was taking up my trousers to put them on, when there was a tap at the door and Severnius appeared with some soft white garments, such as he himself wore, thrown over his arm. In the most delicate manner possible, he conveyed the wish that I might feel disposed to put them on. I blushed, — they seemed such womanish things. He misinterpreted my confusion. He assured me by every means in his power that I was entirely welcome to them, that it would give him untold pleasure to provide for my every want. I could not stand out against such generosity. I reached for the things — swaddling clothes I called them — and Severnius helped me to array myself in them. I happened to glance into the mirror, and I did not recognize myself. I had some sense of how a barbarian must feel in his first civilized suit.

At my friend's suggestion I hung my own familiar apparel up in the closet, — you may imagine with what reluctance.

But I may say, right here, that I grew rapidly to my new clothes. I soon liked them. There was something very graceful in the cut and style of them.

They covered and adorned the body without disguising it. They left the limbs and muscles free and encouraged grace of pose and movement.

The elegant folds in which the garments hung from the shoulders and the waist, the tassels and fringes and artistic drapery arrangements, while seemingly left to their own caprice, were as secure in their place as the plumage of a bird, — which the wind may ruffle but cannot displace.

I suspect that it requires a great deal of skill to construct a Marsian costume, whether for male or female. They are not altogether dissimilar; the women's stuffs are of a little finer quality ordinarily, but their dress is not usually so elaborately trimmed as the men's garb, which struck me as very peculiar. Both sexes wear white, or a soft cream. The fabric is either a sort of fine linen, or a mixture of silk and wool.

After Severnius and I came to understand each other, as comrades and friends, he laughingly compared my dress, in which I had made my first appearance, to the saddle and housings of a horse. He declared that he and his friends were not quite sure whether I was a man or a beast. But he was too polite to give me the remotest hint, during our early acquaintance, that he considered my garb absurd.

When, having completed my toilet, I indicated to him that I was ready for the next thing on the program, — which I sincerely hoped might be breakfast, — he approached me and taking my hand placed a gold ring on my finger. It was set with a superb rubellite enhanced with pearls. The stone was the only bit of color in my entire dress. Even my shoes were of white canvas.

I thanked him as well as I was able for this especial mark of favor. I was pleased that he had given me a gem not only beautiful, but possessing remarkable qualities. I held it in a ray of sunlight and turned it this way and that, to show him that I was capable of appreciating its beauties and its peculiar characteristics.

He was delighted, and I had the satisfaction of feeling that I had made a good impression upon him.

He led the way down-stairs, and luckily into the breakfast room.

We were served by men dressed similarly to ourselves, though their clothing was without trimming and was of coarser material than ours. They moved about the room swiftly and noiselessly. Motion upon that planet seems so natural and so easy. There is very little inertia to overcome.

Our meal was rather odd; it consisted of fruits, some curiously prepared cereals, and a hot, palatable drink, but no meat.

After this light but entirely satisfactory repast we ascended the grand stairway—a marvel of beauty in its elaborate carvings—and entered a lofty apartment occupying a large part of the last *etage*.

I at first made out that it was a place devoted to the fine arts. I had noticed a somewhat conspicuous absence, in the rooms below, of the sort of things with which rich people in our country crowd their houses. I understood now, they were all marshaled up here.

There were exquisitely carved vessels of all descriptions, bronzes, marbles, royal paintings, precious minerals.

Here also were the riches of color.

The brilliant morning light came through the most beautiful windows I have ever seen, even in our finest cathedrals. The large central stained glasses were studded round with prisms that played extraordinary pranks with the sunbeams, which, as they glanced from them, were splintered into a thousand scintillating bits, as splendid as jewels.

We sat down, I filled—I do not know why—with a curious sense of expectancy that was half awe.

Across one end of the great room was stretched a superb curtain of tapestry,—a mosaic in silk and wool.

Severnius did not make any other sign or gesture to me except the one that bade me be seated.

I watched him wonderingly but furtively. He seemed to be composing himself, as I have seen saintly people compose themselves in church. Not that he was saintly; he did not strike me as being that kind of a man, though there was that about him which proclaimed him to be a good man, whose friendship would be a valuable acquisition.

He folded his hands loosely in his lap and sat motionless, his glance resting serenely on one of the great windows for a time and then passing on to other objects equally beautiful.

We were still enwrapped in this august silence when I became conscious that somewhere, afar off, beyond the tapestry curtain, there were stealing toward us strains of unusual, ineffable music, tantalizingly sweet and vague.

Gradually the almost indistinguishable sounds detached themselves from, and rose above, the pulsing silence, — or that unappreciable harmony we call silence, — and swelled up among the arches that ribbed the lofty ceiling, and rolled and reverberated through the great dome above, and came reflected down to us in refined and sublimated undulations.

Our souls — my soul, — in this new wonder and ecstasy I forgot Severnius, — awoke in responsive raptures, inconceivably thrilling and exalted.

I did not need to be told that it was sacred music, it invoked the Divine Presence unmistakably. No influence that had ever before been trained upon my spiritual senses had so compelled to adoration of the Supreme One who holds and rules all worlds.

> "He lifts me to the golden doors;
>     The flashes come and go;
> All heaven bursts her starry floors,
>     And strows her lights below,
> And deepens on and up ! the gates
>     Roll back.   *   *   *   *"

This I murmured, and texts of our scriptures, and fragments of anthems. It was as if I brought my earthly tribute to lay on this Marsian shrine.

The gates did roll back, the heavens were broken up, new spiritual heights were shown to me, up which my spirit mounted. I looked at Severnius. His eyes were closed. His face, lighted as by an inner illumination, and his whole attitude, suggested a "waiting upon God," that

"Intercourse divine,
Which God permits, ordains, across the line."

There stole insensibly upon the sound-burdened air, the hallowed perfume of burning incense.

I conjectured, and truly as I afterward learned, that I was in my friend's private sanctuary. It was his spiritual lavatory, in which he made daily ablutions, a service in which the soul lays aside the forms necessary in public worship and stands unveiled before its God.

It was a rare honor he paid me, in permitting me to accompany him. And he repeated it every morning during my stay in his house, except on one or two occasions. It speedily became almost a necessity to me. You know how it is when you have formed a habit of exercising your muscles in a gymnasium. If you leave it off, you are uncomfortable, you have a feeling that you have cheated your body out of its right. It was so with me, when for any reason I was obliged to forego this higher exercise. I was heavy in spirit, my conscience accused me of a wrong to one of the "selfs" in me, — for we have several selfs, I think.

There was not always music. Sometimes a wonderful voice chanted psalms and praises, and recited poems that troubled the soul's deepest waters. At first I did not understand the words, of course, but the intonations spoke to me the same as music does. And I felt that I knew what the words expressed.

Often there was nothing there but The Presence, which hushed our voices and set our souls in tune with heavenly things. No matter, I was fed and satisfied.

At the end of a sweet half-hour, the music died away, and we rose and passed out of the sacred place. I longed to question Severnius, but was powerless.

He led the way down into the library, which was just off the wide entrance hall. Books were ranged round the walls on shelves, the same as we dispose ours. But they were all bound in white cloth or white leather.

The lettering on the backs was gold.

I took one in my hand and flipped its leaves to show Severnius that I knew what a book was. He was delighted. He asked me, in a language which he and I had speedily established between ourselves, if I would not like to learn the Marsian tongue. I replied that it was what I wished above all things to do. We set to work at once. His teaching was very simple and natural, and I quickly mastered several important principles.

After a little a servant announced some visitors, and Severnisu went out into the hall to receive them. He left the door open, and I saw that the visitors were the astronomers I had met the night before. They asked to see me, and Severnius ushered them into the library. I stood up and shook hands with each one, as he advanced, and repeated their own formula for "How do you do!" which quite amused them. I suppose the words sounded very parrot-like, — I did not know where to put the accent. They congratulated me with many smiles and gesticulations on my determination to learn the language, —Severnius having explained this fact to them. He also told them that I had perhaps better be left to myself and him until I had mastered it, when of course I should be much more interesting to them and they to me.

They acquiesced, and with many bows and waves of the hand, withdrew.

The language, I found, was not at all difficult, — not so arbitrary as many of our modern languages. It was similar in form and construction to the ancient languages of southern Europe. The proper names had an almost familiar sound. That of the country I was in was Paleveria. The city was called Thursia, and there was a river flowing through it, — one portion of Severnius' grounds, at the back of the house, sloped to it, — named the Gyro.

# CHAPTER 2.

## A WOMAN.

"Her face so fair, as flesh it seemed not,
But hevenly portrait of bright angels hew,
Clear as the skye withouten blame or blot,
Through goodly mixture of complexion's dew;
And in her cheeks the vermeil red did shew
Like roses in a bed of lilies shed.

   *     *     *     *     *     *

In her faire eyes two living lamps did flame."
                         — SPENSER.

Thus far, I had seen no women. I was curious on this point, and I was not kept long in suspense. Late in the afternoon of the day following my arrival, Severnius and I went out to walk about the grounds, and were returning through an avenue of eucalyptus trees, — of a variety more wide-spreading in their branches than any I have seen in our country, — when a person alighted from a carriage in the *porte cochere* and, instead of entering the house, came to meet us. It was a woman. Though it was not left to her dress, nor her stature, — she was nearly as tall as myself, — to proclaim that fact; her grace and carriage would have determined her sex, if her beautiful face had not. She advanced swiftly, with long, free steps. Her white dress, similar in cut and style to ours, was relieved only by a girdle studded with gems. She carried a little white parasol with a gold fringe, and wore no head-gear to crush down her beautifully massed hair.

I felt myself growing red under her lively gaze, and attributed it to my clothes. I was not accustomed to them yet, and I felt as you would to appear before a beautiful woman in your night shirt. Especially if you fancied you saw something in her eyes which made you suspect that she thought you cut a ludicrous figure. Of course that was my imagination; my apparel, in her eyes, must have been correct, since it was selected from among his best by my new friend, who was unmistakably a man of taste.

Her face, which was indescribably lovely, was also keenly intelligent, — that sort of intelligence which lets nothing escape, which is as quick to grasp a humorous situation as a sublime truth. It was a face of power and of passion, — of, I might say, manly self-restraint, — but yet so soft!

I now observed for the first time the effect of the pinkish atmosphere on the complexion. You have seen ladies in a room where the light came through crimson hangings or glass stained red. So it was here.

Severnius smiled, spoke, and gave her his hand. The glance they bestowed upon each other established their relationship in my mind instantly. I had seen that glance a thousand times, without suspecting it had ever made so strong an impression upon me that in a case like this I should accept its evidence without other testimony. They were brother and sister. I was glad of that, for the reason, I suppose, that every unmarried man is glad to find a beautiful woman unmarried, — there are seductive possibilities in the situation.

Severnius did his best to introduce us. He called her Elodia. I learned afterwards that ladies and gentlemen in that country have no perfunctory titles, like Mrs., or Mr., they support their dignity without that. It would have seemed belittling to say "Miss" Elodia.

I had a feeling that she did not attach much importance to me, that she was half amused at the idea of me; a peculiar tilting-up of her eyebrows told me so, and I was piqued. It seemed unfair that, simply because she could not account for me, she should set me down as inferior, or impossible, or ridiculous, whichever was in her mind. She regarded me as I have sometimes regarded un-English foreigners in the streets of New York.

She indulged her curiosity about me only for a moment, asking a few questions I inferred, and then passed me over as though she had more weighty matters in hand. I knew, later on, that she waived me as a topic of conversation when her brother insisted upon talking about me, saying half impatiently, "Wait till he can talk and explain himself, Severnius, — since you say he is going to learn our speech."

I studied her with deep interest as we walked along, and no movement or accent of hers was lost upon me. Once she raised her hand — her wide sleeve slipped back and bared a lovely arm — to break off a long scimeter-shaped leaf from a bough overhead. Quicker than thought I sprang at the bough and snapped off the leaf in advance of her, and presented it with a low obeisance. She drew herself up with a look of indignant surprise, but instantly relented as though to a person whose eccentricities, for some reason or other, might better be excused. She did not, however, take the leaf, — it fluttered to the ground.

She was not like any other woman, — any woman I had ever seen before. You could not accuse her of hauteur, yet she bore

herself like a royal personage, though with no suggestion of af-
fecting that sort of an air. You had to take her as seriously as
you would the Czar. I saw this in her brother's attitude toward
her. There was none of that condescension in his manner that
there often is in our manner toward the women of our house-
holds. I began to wonder whether she might not be the queen
of the realm! But she was not. She was simply a private citizen.

She sat at the dinner table with us, and divided the honors
equally with Severnius.

I wish I could give you an idea of that dinner, — the dining-
room, the service, the whole thing! It surpassed my finest con-
ceptions of taste and elegance.

We sat down not merely to eat, — though I was hungry
enough! — but to enjoy ourselves in other ways.

There was everything for the eye to delight in. The room
was rich in artistic decorations upon which the rarest talent must
have been employed. The table arrangements were superb; gold
and silver, crystal, fine china, embroidered linen, flowers. And
the food, served in many courses, was a happy combination of
the substantial and the delicate. There was music — not too near
— of a bright and lively character. Music enters largely into the
life of these people. It seemed to me that something beat time
to almost everything we did.

The conversation carried on between the brother and sister —
in which I could take no more part than a deaf-mute — was, I
felt sure, extremely entertaining if not important. My eyes served
me well, — for one sense is quick to assume the burdens of another, — and I knew that the talk was not mere banter, nor was
it simply the necessary exchange of words and opinions about
everyday matters which must take place in families periodically,
concerning fuel, and provisions, and servants, and water-tax, and

the like. It took a much higher range. The faces of both were animated, their eyes beamed brightly upon each other. It was clear that the brother did not talk down to her understanding, rather he talked up to it, — or no, they were on a level with each other, the highest level of both, for they held each other up to their best. However, Elodia had been away for a couple of days, I learned, and absence gives a bloom of newness which it is delightful to brush off.

I did not detect any of the quality we call chivalry in Severnius' pose, nor of its complement in hers. Though one would hardly expect that between brothers and sisters anywhere. Still, we have a way with our near women relations which never ignores the distinction between the sexes; we humor them, patronize them, tyrannize over them. And they defer to, and exalt us, and usually acknowledge our superiority.

It was not so with this pair. They respected and honored each other equally. And there was a charming *camaraderie* between them, the same as if they had both been men — or women, if you single out the right kind.

They held widely different opinions upon many subjects, but they never crowded them upon each other. Their tastes were dissimilar. For one thing, Elodia had not her brother's fine religious sense. She seldom entered the sanctuary, though once or twice I saw her there, seated far apart from Severnius and myself.

Stimulated by the hope of some day being able to talk with her, and of convincing her that I was a person not altogether beneath her intelligence, I devoted myself, mind and soul, to the Paleverian language. In six weeks I could read and write it fairly well.

Severnius was untiring in his teaching; and every day strengthened my regard for him as a man. He was an accomplished scholar, and he was as clean-souled as a child, — but not weakly or ignorantly so. He knew evil as well as good; but he renounced the one and accepted the other He was a man "appointed by Almighty God to stand for a fact." And I never knew him to weaken his position by defending it. Often we spent hours in the observatory together. It was a glorious thing to me to watch the splendid fleet of asteroids sailing between Jupiter and Mars, and to single out the variously colored moons of Jupiter, and to distinguish with extraordinary clearness a thousand other wonders but dimly seen from the Earth.

Even to study the moons of Mars, the lesser one whirling round the planet with such astonishing velocity, was a world of entertainment to me.

I had begged Severnius not to ask to me see any visitors at all until I could acquit myself creditably in conversation. He agreed, and I saw no one. I believe that in those weeks of quiet study, observation, and close companionship of one noble man, my soul was cleared of much dross. I lived with books, Severnius, and the stars.

At last, I no longer feared to trust myself to speak, even to Elodia. It was a great surprise to her, and evidently a pleasure too.

My first brilliant attempt was at the dinner table. Severnius adriotly drew me into a conversation about our world. Elodia turned her delightful gaze upon me so frankly and approvingly that I felt myself blushing like a boy whom his pretty Sabbath-school teacher praises with her smile when he says his text.

Up to that time, although she had been polite to me, — so entirely polite that I never for a moment felt myself an intruder in her home, — she apparently took no great interest in me. But now she voluntarily addressed me whenever we met, and took pains to draw me out.

Once she glanced at a book I was reading, a rather heavy work, and smiled.

"You have made astonishing progress," she said.

"I have had the best of instructors," I replied.

"Ah, yes; Severnius has great patience. And besides, he likes you. And then of course he is not wholly disinterested, he wants to hear about your planet."

"And do you?" I asked foolishly. I wanted somehow to get the conversation to running in a personal channel.

"O, of course," she returned indifferently, "though I am not an astronomer. I should like to hear something about your people."

I took that cue joyfully, and soon we were on very sociable terms with each other. She listened to my stories and descriptions with a most flattering interest, and I soon found myself worshiping her as a goddess. Yes, as a goddess, not a woman. Her entire lack of coquetry prevented me from making love to her, or would have prevented me if I had dared to have such a thought. If there could have been anything tender between us, I think she must have made the advances. But this is foolish. I am merely trying to give you some idea of the kind of woman she was. But I know that I cannot do that; the quality of a woman must be felt to be understood.

There was a great deal of social gayety in Thursia. We went out frequently, to operas, to concerts, and to crowded gatherings in splendid homes. I observed that Elodia immediately became the centre of interest wherever she appeared. She gave fresh zest to every amusement or conversation. She seemed to dignify with her presence whatever happened to be going on, and made it worth while. Not that she distinguished herself in speech or act; she had the effect of being infinitely greater than anything she did or said and one was always looking out for manifestations of that. She kept one's interest in her up to the highest pitch. I often asked myself, "Why is it that we are always looking at her with a kind of inquiry in our glances?—what is it that we expect her to do?"

It was a great part of her charm that she was not *blasé*. She was full of interest in all about her, she was keenly and delightfully alive. Her manners were perfect, and yet she seemed careless of etiquette and conventions. Her good manners were a part of herself, as her regal carriage was.

It was her unvarying habit, almost, to spend several hours down town every day. I ventured to ask Severnius wherefore.

He replied that she had large business interests, and looked carefully after them herself.

I expressed astonishment, and Severnius was equally surprised at me. I questioned him and he explained.

"My father was a banker," he said, "and very rich. My sister inherited his gift and taste for finance. I took after my mother's family, who were scientists. We were trained, of course, in our early years according to our respective talents. At our parents' death we inherited their fortune in equal shares. Elodia was prepared to take up my father's business where he left it. In fact he had associated her with himself in the business for some time previous to his departure, and she has carried it on very successfully ever since."

"She is a banker!" said I.

"Yes. I, myself, have always had a liking for astronomy, and I have been employed, ever since I finished my education, in the State Observatory."

"And how do you employ your capital?" I asked.

"Elodia manages it for me. It is all in the bank, or in investments which she makes. I use my dividends largely in the interest of science. The State does a great deal in that direction, but not enough."

"And what, may I ask, does she do with her surplus, — your sister, I mean, — she must make a great deal of money?"

"She re-invests it. She has a speculative tendency, and is rather daring; though they tell me she is very safe — far-sighted, or large-sighted, I should call it. I do not know how many great enterprises she is connected with, — railroads, lines of steamers, mining and manufacturing operations. And besides, she is public-spirited. She is much interested in the cause of education, — practical education for the poor especially. She is president of the school board here in the city, and she is also a member of the city council. A great many of our modern improvements are due to her efforts."

My look of amazement arrested his attention.

"Why are you so surprised?" he asked. "Do not your women engage in business?"

"Well, not to such an extraordinary degree," I replied. "We have women who work in various ways, but there are very few of them who have large business interests, and they are not entrusted with important public affairs, such as municipal government and the management of schools!"

"Oh!" returned Severnius with the note of one who does not quite understand. "Would you mind telling me why? Is it because they are incapable, or — unreliable?"

Neither of the words he chose struck me pleasantly as applied to my countrywomen. I remembered that I was the sole representative of the Earth on Mars, and that it stood me in hand to be careful about the sort of impressions I gave out. It was as if I were on the witness' stand, under oath. Facts must tell the story, not opinions, — though personally I have great confidence in my opinions. I thought of our government departments where women are the experts, and of their almost spotless record for faithfulness and honesty, and replied:

"They are both capable and reliable, in as far as they have had experience. But their chances have been circumscribed, and I believe they lack the inclination to assume grave public duties. I fear I cannot make you understand, — our women are so different, so unlike your sister."

Elodia was always my standard of comparison.

"Perhaps you men take care of them all," suggested Severnius, "and they have grown dependent. We have some such women here."

"No, I do not think it is that entirely," said I. "For in my city alone, more than a hundred and seventy thousand women support not only themselves, but others who are dependent upon them."

"Ah, indeed! but how?"

"By work."

"You mean servants?"

"Not so-called. I mean intelligent, self-respecting women; teachers, clerks, stenographers, type-writers."

"I should think it would be more agreeable, and easier, for them to engage in business as our women do."

"No doubt it would," I replied, feeling myself driven to a close scrutiny of the Woman Question, as we call it, for the first time in my life. For I saw that my friend was deeply interested and wanted to get at the literal truth. "But the women of my country," I went on, "the self-supporting ones, do not have control of money. They have a horror of speculation, and shrink from taking risks and making ventures, the failure of which would mean loss or ruin to others. A woman's right to make her living is restricted to the powers within herself, powers of brain and hand. She is a beginner, you know. She has not yet learned to make money by the labor of others; she does not know how to manipulate those who are less intelligent and less capable than herself, and to turn their ignorance and helplessness to her own account. Perhaps I had better add that she is more religious than man, and is sustained in this seeming injustice by something she calls conscience."

Severnius was silent for a moment; he had a habit of setting his reason to work and searching out explanations in his own mind, of things not easily understood.

As a rule, the Marsians have not only very highly developed physical faculties, such as sight and hearing, but remarkably acute intellects. They let no statement pass without examination, and they scrutinize facts closely and seek for causes.

"If so many women," said he, "are obliged to support themselves and others beside, as you say, by their work simply, they must receive princely wages,—and of course they have no responsibilities, which is a great saving of energy."

I remembered having heard it stated that in New York City, the United States Bureau gives the average of women's wages— leaving out domestic service and unskilled labor—as five dollars and eighty-five cents per week. I mentioned the fact, and Severnius looked aghast.

"What, a mere pittance!" said he. "Only about a third as much as I give my stableman. But then the conditions are different, no doubt. Here in Thursia that would no more than fight off the wolf, as we say,—the hunger and cold. It would afford no taste of the better things, freedom, leisure, recreation, but would reduce life to its lowest terms,—mere existence."

"I fear the conditions are much the same with us," I replied.

"And do your women submit to such conditions,—do they not try to alter them, throw them off?"

"They submit, of course," I said; "I never heard of a revolt or an insurrection among them! Though there seems to be growing up among them, lately, a determination strong as death, to work out of those conditions as fast as may be. They realize— just as men have been forced to realize in this century—that work of the hands cannot compete with work of machines, and that trained brains are better capital than trained fingers. So, slowly but surely, they are reaching up to the higher callings and working into places of honor and trust. The odds are against them, because the 'ins' always have a tremendous advantage over the 'outs.' The women, having never been in, must submit to a rigid examination and extraordinary tests. They know that, and they are rising to it. Whenever, it is said, they come into competition with men, in our colleges and training schools, they hold their own and more."

"What are they fitting for?" asked Severnius.

"Largely for the professions. They are becoming doctors, lawyers, editors, artists, writers. The enormous systems of public schools in my own and other countries is entirely in their hands,— except of course in the management and directorship."

"Except in the management and directorship?" echoed Severnius.

"Of course they do not provide and disburse the funds, see to the building of school-houses, and dictate the policy of the schools!" I retorted. "But they teach them; you can hardly find a male teacher except at the head of a school,—to keep the faculty in order."

Severnius refrained from comment upon this, seeing, I suppose, that I was getting a little impatient. He walked along with his head down. I think I neglected to say that we were taking a long tramp into the country, as we often did. In order to change the conversation, I asked him what sort of a government they had in Paleveria, and was delighted when he replied that it was a free republic.

"My country is a republic also," I said, proudly.

"We both have much to be thankful for," he answered. "A republic is the only natural government in the world, and man cannot get above nature."

I thought this remark rather singular, — at variance with progress and high civilization. But I let it pass, thinking to take it up at some future time.

"How do you vote here?" I asked. "What are your qualifications and restrictions?"

"Briefly told," he replied. "Every citizen may vote on all public questions, and in all elections."

"But what constitutes citizenship?"

"A native-born is a citizen when he or she reaches maturity. Foreigners are treated as minors until they have lived as long under the government as it takes for a child to come of age. It is thus," he added, facetiously, "that we punish people for presuming to be born outside our happy country."

"Excuse me," I said, "but do I understand you to say that your women have the right of suffrage?"

"Assuredly. Do not yours?"

"Indeed no!" I replied, the masculine instinct of superiority swelling within me.

Severnius wears spectacles. He adjusted them carefully on his nose and looked at me.

"But did you not tell me just now that your country is a republic?"

"It is, but we do not hold that women are our political equals,"
I answered.

His face was an exclamation and interrogation point fused
into one.

"Indeed! and how do you manage it, — how, for instance, can
you prevent them from voting?"

"O, they don't often try it," I said, laughing. "When they do,
we simply throw their ballots out of the count."

"Is it possible! That seems to me a great unfairness. However, it can be accounted for, I suppose, from the fact that things
are so different on the Earth to what they are here. Our government, you see, rests upon a system of taxation. We tax all
property to defray governmental expenses, and for many other
purposes tending toward the general good; which makes it necessary that all our citizens shall have a voice in our political economy. But you say your women have no property, and so —"

"I beg your pardon!" I interposed; "I did not say that. We
have a great many very rich women, — women whose husbands
or fathers have left them fortunes."

"Then they of course have a vote?"

"They do not. You can't make a distinction like that."

"No? But you exempt their property, perhaps?"

"Of course not."

"Do you tell me that you tax property, to whatever amount,
and for whatever purpose, you choose, without allowing the owner
her fractional right to decide about either the one or the other?"

"Their interests are identical with ours," I replied, "so what
is the difference? We men manage the government business, and
I fancy we do it sufficiently well."

I expanded my chest after this remark, and Severnius simply looked at me. I think that at that moment I suffered vicariously in his scornful regard for all my countrymen.

I did not like the Socratic method he had adopted in this conversation, and I turned the tables on him.

"Do your women hold office, other than in the school board and the council?" I asked.

"O, yes, fully half our offices are filled by women."

"And you make no discrimination in the kind of office?"

"The law makes none; those things adjust themselves. Fitness, equipment, are the only things considered. A woman, the same as a man, is governed by her taste and inclination in the matter of officeholding. Do women never take a hand in state affairs on the Earth?"

"Yes, in some countries they do, — monarchies. There have been a good many women sovereigns. There are a few now."

"And are they successful rulers?"

"Some are, some are not."

"The same as men. That proves that your women are not really inferior."

"Well, I should say not!" I retorted. "Our women are very superior; we treat them more as princesses than as inferiors, — they are angels."

I was carried away in the heat of resentment, and knew that what I had said was half cant.

"I beg your pardon!" said Severnius quickly; "I got a wrong impression from your statements. I fear I am very stupid. Are they all angels?"

I gave him a furtive glance and saw that he was in earnest. His brows were drawn together with a puzzled look.

I had a sudden vision of a scene in Five Points; several groups of frowsled, petticoated beings, laughing, joking, swearing, quarreling, fighting, and drinking beer from dirty mugs.

"No, not all of them," I replied, smiling. "That was a figure of speech. There are so many classes."

"Let us confine our discussion to one, then," he returned. "To the women who might be of your own family; that will simplify matters. And now tell me, please, how this state of things came about, this subjection of a part of your people. I cannot understand it, — these subjects being of your own flesh and blood. I should think it would breed domestic discontent, where some of the members of a family wield a power and enjoy a privilege denied to the others. Fancy my shaking a ballot over Elodia's head!"

"O, Elodia!" I said, and was immediately conscious that my accent was traitorous to my countrywomen. I made haste to add,

"Your sister is — incomparable. She is unusual even here. I have seen none others like her."

"How do you mean?"

"I mean that she is as responsible as a man; she is not inconsequent."

"Are your women inconsequent?"

"They have been called so, and we think it rather adds to their attractiveness. You see they have always been relieved of responsibility, and I assure you the large majority of them have no desire to assume it, — I mean in the matter of government and politics."

"Yes?"

I dislike an interrogative "yes," and I made no reply. Severnius added,

"I suppose they have lost the faculty which you say they lack, — the faculty that makes people responsible, — through disuse. I have seen the same thing in countries on the other side of our globe, where races have been held as slaves for several centuries. They seem to have no ideas about personal rights, or liberties, as pertaining to themselves, and no inclination in that direction. It always struck me as being the most pathetic feature of their condition that they and everybody else accepted it as a matter of course, as they would a law of nature. In the place of strength and self-assertion there has come to them a dumb patience, or an unquestioning acquiescence like that of people born blind. Are your women happy?"

"You should see them!" I exclaimed, with certain ball-room memories rushing upon me, and visions of fair faces radiant with the joy of living. But these were quickly followed by other pictures, and I felt bound to add, "Of late, a restless spirit has developed in certain circles, — "

"The working circles, I suppose," interrupted Severnius. "You spoke of the working women getting into the professions."

"Not those exclusively. Even the women of leisure are not so satisfied as they used to be. There has been, for a great many years, more or less chaffing about women's rights, but now they are beginning to take the matter seriously."

"Ah, they are waking up, perhaps?"

"Yes, some of them are waking up, — a good many of them. It is a little ridiculous, when one thinks of it, seeing they have no power to enforce their 'rights', and can never attain them except through the condescension of men. Tell me, Severnius, when did your women wake up?"

Severnius smiled. "My dear sir, I think they have never been asleep!"

We stalked along silently for a time; the subject passed out of my mind, or was driven out by the beauties of the landscape about us. I was especially impressed with the magnificence of the trees that hedged every little patch of farm land, and threw their protecting arms around houses and cottages, big and little; and with the many pellucid streams flowing naturally, or divided like strands of silk and guided in new courses, to lave the roots of trees or run through pasture lands where herds were feeding.

A tree is something to be proud of in Paleveria, more than a fine residence; more even than ancient furniture and cracked china. Perhaps because the people sit out under their trees a great deal, and the shade of them has protected the heads of many generations, and they have become hallowed through sacred memories and traditions. In Paleveria they have tree doctors, whose business it is to ward off disease, heal wounded or broken boughs, and exterminate destructive insects.

Severnius startled me suddenly with another question:

"What, may I ask, is your theory of Man's creation?"

"God made Man, and from one of his ribs fashioned woman," I replied catechetically.

"Ours is different, said he. "It is this: A pair of creatures, male and female, sprang simultaneously from an enchanted lake in the mountain region of a country called Caskia, in the northern part of this continent. They were only animals, but they were beautiful and innocent. God breathed a Soul into them and they were Man and Woman, equals in all things."

"A charming legend!" said I.

Later on I learned the full breadth of the meaning of the equality he spoke of. At that time it was impossible for me to comprehend it, and I can only convey it to you in a complete account of my further experiences on that wonderful planet.

# CHAPTER 3.

It was winter, and snow was on the ground; white and sparkling, and as light as eider-down. Elodia kept a fine stable. Four magnificent white horses were harnessed to her sleigh, which was in the form of an immense swan, with a head and neck of frosted silver. The body of it was padded outside with white varnished leather, and inside with velvet of the color of a dove's breast. The robes were enormous skins of polar bears, lined with a soft, warm fabric of wool and silk. The harness was bestrung with little silver bells of most musical and merry tone; and all the trappings and accoutrements were superb. Elodia had luxurious tastes, and indulged them.

Every day we took an exhilarating drive. The two deep, comfortable seats faced each other like seats in a landau. Severnius and I occupied one, and Elodia the other; so that I had the pleasure of looking at her whenever I chose, and of meeting her eyes in conversation now and then, which was no small part of my enjoyment. The mere sight of her roused the imagination and quickened the pulse. Her eyes were unusually dark, but they had blue rays, and were as clear and beautiful as agates held under water. In fact they seemed to swim in an invisible liquid. Her complexion had the effect of alabaster through which a pink light

shines, — deepest in the cheeks, as though they were more transparent than the rest of her face. Her head, crowned with a fascinating little cap, rose above her soft furs like a regal flower.
She was so beautiful that I wondered at myself that I could bear
the sight of her.

Strange to say, the weather was not cold, it was simply brac-
ing, — hardly severe enough to make the ears tingle.

The roads were perfect everywhere, and we often drove into
the country. The horses flew over the wide white stretches at an
incredible speed.

One afternoon when, at the usual hour, the coachman rang
the bell and announced that he was ready, I was greatly disappointed to find that we were not to have Elodia. But I said nothing, for I was shy about mentioning her name.

When we were seated, Severnius gave directions to the driver.

"Time yourself, Giddo, so that you will be at the Public Square
at precisely three o'clock," said he, and turned to me. "We shall
want to see the parade."

"What parade?" I inquired.

"Oh! has not Elodia told you? This is The Auroras' Annual, —
a great day. The parade will be worth seeing."

In the excitement of the drive, and in my disappointment
about not having Elodia with us, I had almost forgotten about
The Auroras' Annual, when three o'clock came. I had seen pa-
rades in New York City, until the spectacle had calloused my sense
of the magnificent, and I very much doubted whether Mars had
anything new to offer me in that line.

Punctual to the minute, Giddo fetched up at the Square, —
among a thousand or so of other turnouts, — with such a flourish
as all Jehus love. We were not a second too soon. There was a
sudden burst of music, infinitely mellowed by distance; and as

far up the street as the eye could well reach there appeared a mounted procession, advancing slowly. Every charger was snow white, with crimped mane and tail, long and flowing, and with trappings of various colors magnificent in silver blazonry.

The musicians only were on foot. They were beating upon drums and blowing transcendent airs through silver wind instruments. I do not know whether it was some quality of the atmosphere that made the strains so ravishing, but they swept over one's soul with a rapture that was almost painful. I could hardly sit still, but I was held down by the thought that if I should get up I would not know what to do. It is a peculiar sensation.

On came the resplendent column with slow, majestic movement; and I unconsciously kept time with the drums, with Browning's stately lines on my tongue, but unspoken:

"Steady they step adown the slope,
Steady they climb the hill."

There was no hill, but a very slight descent. As they drew nearer the splendor of the various uniforms dazzled my eyes. You will remember that everything about us was white; the buildings all of white stone or brick, the ground covered with snow, and the crowds of people lining the streets all dressed in the national color, or no-color.

There were several companies in the procession, and each company wore distinguishing badges and carried flags and banners peculiar to itself.

The housings on the horses of the first brigade were of yellow, and all the decorations of the riders corresponded; of the second pale blue, and of the third sky-pink. The uniforms of the riders were inconceivably splendid; fantastic and gorgeous headgear, glittering belts, silken scarfs and sashes, badges and medals flashing with gems, and brilliant colors twisted into strange and curious devices.

As the first division was about to pass, I lost my grip on myself and half started to my feet with a smothered exclamation, "Elodia!"

Severnius put out his hand as though he were afraid I was going to leap out of the sleigh, or do something unusual.

"What is it?" he cried, and following my gaze he added, "Yes, that is Elodia in front; she is the Supreme Sorceress of the Order of the Auroras."

"The — *what!*"

"Don't be frightened," he laughed; "the word means nothing, — it is only a title."

I could not believe him when I looked at the advancing figure of Elodia. She sat her horse splendidly erect. Her fair head was crowned with a superb diadem of gold and topazes, with a diamond star in the centre, shooting rays like the sun. Her expression was grave and lofty; she glanced neither to right nor left, but gazed straight ahead — at nothing, or at something infinitely beyond mortal vision. Her horse champed its bits, arched its beautiful neck, and stepped with conscious pride; dangling the gold fringe on its sheeny yellow satin saddle-cloth, until one could hardly bear the sight.

"The words mean nothing!" I repeated to myself. "It is not so; Severnius has deceived me. His sister is a sorceress; a — I don't know what! But no woman could preserve that majestic mien, that proud solemnity of countenance, if she were simply — playing! There is a mystery here."

I scrutinized every rider as they passed. There was not a man among them, — all women. Their faces had all borrowed, or had tried to borrow, Elodia's queenly look. Many of them only burlesqued it. None were as beautiful as she.

When it was all over, and the music had died away in the distance, we drove off, — Giddo threading his way with consummate skill, which redounded much to his glory in certain circles he cared for, through the crowded thoroughfares.

I could not speak for many minutes, and Severnius was a man upon whom silence always fell at the right time. I never knew him to break in upon another's mood for his own entertainment. Nor did he spy upon your thoughts; he left you free. By-and-by, I appealed to him:

"Tell me, Severnius, what does it mean?"

"This celebration?" returned he. "With pleasure. Giddo, you may drive round for half an hour, and then take us to the Auroras' Temple, — it is open to visitors to-day."

We drew the robes closely, and settled ourselves more comfortably, as we cleared the skirts of the crowd. It was growing late and the air was filled with fine arrows of frost, touched by the last sunbeams, — their sharp little points stinging our faces as we were borne along at our usual lively speed.

"This society of the Auroras," said Severnius," originated several centuries ago, in the time of a great famine. In those days the people were poor and improvident, and a single failure in their crops left them in a sorry condition. Some of the wealthiest women of the country banded themselves together and worked systematically for the relief of the sufferers. Their faces appeared so beautiful, and beamed with such a light of salvation as they went about from hut to hut, that they got the name of 'auroras' among the simple poor. And they banished want and hunger so magically, that they were also called 'sorcerers'."

"O, then, it is a charitable organization?" I exclaimed, much relieved.

"It was," replied Severnius. "It was in active operation for a hundred or so years. Finally, when there was no more need of it, the State having undertaken the care of its poor, it passed into a sentiment, such as you have seen to-day."

"A very costly and elaborate sentiment," I retorted.

"Yes, and it is growing more so, all the time," said he. "I sometimes wonder where it is going to stop! For those who, like Elodia, have plenty of money, it does not matter; but some of the women we saw in those costly robes and ornaments can ill afford them, — they mean less of comfort in their homes and less of culture to their children."

"I should think their husbands would not allow such a waste of money," I said, forgetting the social economy of Mars.

"It does not cost any more than membership in the orders to which the husbands themselves belong," returned he. "They argue, of course, that they need the recreation, and also that membership in such high-toned clubs gives them and their children a better standing and greater influence in society."

Severnius did not forget his usual corollary, — the question with which he topped out every explanation he made about his country and people.

"Have you nothing of the sort on the Earth?" he asked.

"Among the women? — we have not," I answered.

"I did not specify," he said.

"O, well, the men have," I admitted; "I belong to one such organization myself, — the City Guards."

"And you guard the city?"

"No; there is nothing to guard it against at present. It's a 'sentiment,' as you say."

"And do you parade?"

"Yes, of course, upon occasion, — there are certain great anniversaries in our nation's history when we appear."

"And why not your women?"

I smiled to myself, as I tried to fancy some of the New York ladies I knew, arrayed in gorgeous habiliments for an equestrian exhibition on Broadway. I replied,

"Really, Severnius, the idea is entirely new to me. I think they would regard it as highly absurd."

"Do they regard you as absurd?" he asked, in that way of his which I was often in doubt about, not knowing whether he was in earnest or not.

"I'm sure I do not know," I said. "They may, — our women have a keen relish for the ludicrous. Still, I cannot think that they do; they appear to look upon us with pride. And they present us with an elaborate silken banner about once a year, stitched together by their own fair fingers and paid for out of their own pocket money. That does not look as though they were laughing at us exactly."

I said this as much to convince myself as Severnius.

The half-hour was up and we were at the Temple gate. The building, somewhat isolated, reared itself before us, a grand conception in chiseled marble, glinting in the brilliant lights shot upon it from various high points. Already it was dark beyond the radius of these lights, — neither of the moons having yet appeared.

Severnius dismissed the sleigh, saying that we would walk home, — the distance was not far, — and we entered the grounds and proceeded to mount the flight of broad steps leading up to the magnificent arched entrance. The great carved doors, — the carvings were emblematic, — swung back and admitted us. The

Temple was splendidly illuminated within, and imagination could not picture anything more imposing than the great central hall and winding stairs, visible all the way up to the dome.

Below, on one side of this lofty hall, there were extensive and luxurious baths. Severnius said the members of the Order were fond of congregating here, — and I did not wonder at that; nothing that appertains to such an establishment was lacking. Chairs and sofas that we would call "Turkish," thick, soft rugs and carpets, pictures, statuary, mirrors, growing plants, rare flowers, books, musical instruments. And Severnius told me the waters were delightful for bathing.

The second story consisted of a series of spacious rooms divided from each other by costly portieres, into which the various emblems and devices were woven in their proper tinctures.

All of these rooms were as sumptuously furnished as those connected with the baths; and the decorations, I thought, were even more beautiful, of a little higher or finer order.

In one of the rooms a lady was playing upon an instrument resembling a harp. She dropped her hands from the strings and came forward graciously.

"Perhaps we are intruding?" said Severnius.

"Ah, no, indeed," she laughed, pleasantly; "no one could be more welcome here than the brother of our Supreme Sorceress!"

"Happy the man who has a distinguished sister!" returned he.

"I am unfortunate," she answered with a slight blush. "Severnius is always welcome for his own sake."

He acknowledged the compliment, and with a certain reluctance, I thought, said, "Will you allow me, Claris, to introduce my friend — from another planet?"

She took a swift step toward me and held out her hand.

"I have long had a great curiosity to meet you, sir," she said.

I bowed low over her hand and murmured that her curiosity could not possibly equal the pleasure I felt in meeting her.

She gave Severnius a quick, questioning look. I believe she thought he had told me something about her. He let her think what she liked.

"How is it you are here?" he asked.

"You mean instead of being with the others?" she returned. "I have not been well lately, and I thought—or my husband thought—I had better not join the procession. I am awaiting them here."

As she spoke, I noticed that she was rather delicate looking. She was tall and slight, with large, bright eyes, and a transparent complexion. If Elodia had not filled all space in my consciousness I think I should have been considerably interested in her. I liked her frank, direct way of meeting us and talking to us. We soon left her and continued our explorations.

I wanted to ask Severnius something about her, but I thought he avoided the subject. He told me, however, that her husband, Massilia, was one of his closest friends. And then he added, "I wonder that she took his advice!"

"Why so," I asked; "do not women here ever take their husbands' advice?"

"Claris is not in the habit of doing so," he returned with, I thought, some severity. And then he immediately spoke of something else quite foreign to her.

The third and last story comprised an immense hall or assembly room, and rows of deep closets for the robes and paraphernalia of the members of the Order. In one of these closets a skeleton was suspended from the ceiling and underneath it stood a coffin. On a shelf were three skulls with their accompanying cross-bones, and several cruel-looking weapons.

Severnius said he supposed these hideous tokens were employed in the initiation of new members. It seemed incredible. I thought that, if it were so, the Marsian women must have stronger nerves than ours.

A great many beautiful marble columns and pillars supported the roof of the hall, and the walls had a curiously fluted appearance. There was a great deal of sculpture, not only figures, but flowers, vines, and all manner of decorations,—even draperies chiseled in marble that looked like frozen lace, with an awful stillness in their ghostly folds. There was a magnificent canopied throne on an elevation like an old-fashioned pulpit, and seats for satellites on either side, and at the base. If I had been alone, I would have gone up and knelt down before the throne,—for of course that was where Elodia sat,—and I would have kissed the yellow cushion on which her feet were wont to rest when she wielded her jeweled scepter. The scepter, I observed, lay on the throne-chair.

There was an orchestra, and there were "stations" for the various officials, and the walls were adorned with innumerable cabalistic insignia. I asked Severnius if he knew the meaning of any of them.

"How should I know?" he replied in surprise. "Only the initiates understand those things."

"Then these women keep their secrets," said I.

"Yes, to be sure they do," he replied.

The apartment to the right, on the entrance floor, opposite the baths, was the last we looked into, and was a magnificent banquet hall. A servant who stood near the door opened it as though it had been the door of a shrine, and no wonder! It was a noble room in its dimensions and in all unparalleled adornments and appurtenances.

The walls and ceiling bristled with candelabra all alight. The tables, set for a banquet, held everything that could charm the eye or tempt the appetite in such a place.

I observed a great many inverted stemglasses of various exquisite styles and patterns, including the thin, flaring goblets, as delicate as a lily-cup, which mean the same thing to Marsians as to us.

"Do these women drink champagne at their banquets?" I asked, with a frown.

"O, yes," replied Severnius. "A banquet would be rather tame without, wouldn't it? The Auroras are not much given to drink, ordinarily, but on occasions like this they are liable to indulge pretty freely."

"Is it possible!" I could say no more than this, and Severnius went on:

"The Auroras, you see, are the cream of our society, — the *elite*, —and costly drinks are typical, in a way, of the highest refinement. Do you people never drink wine at your social gatherings?"

"The men do, of course, but not the women," I replied in a tone which the whole commonwealth of Paleveria might have taken as a rebuke.

"Ah, I fear I shall never be able to understand!" said he. "It is very confusing to my mind, this having two codes — social as well as political — to apply separately to members of an identical community. I don't see how you can draw the line so sharply. It is like having two distinct currents in a river-bed. Don't the waters ever get mixed?"

"You are facetious," I returned, coldly.

"No, really, I am in earnest," said he. "Do no women in your country ever do these things, — parade and drink wine, and the like, — which you say you men are not above doing?"

I replied with considerable energy:

"I have never before to-day seen women of any sort dress themselves up in conspicuous uniforms and exhibit themselves publicly for the avowed purpose of being seen and making a sensation, except in circuses. And circus women, —well, they don't count. And of course we have a class of women who crack champagne bottles and even quaff other fiery liquors as freely as men, but I do not need to tell you what kind of creatures those are."

At that moment there were sounds of tramping feet outside, and the orchestra filed in at the farther end of the *salon* and took their places on a high dais. At a given signal every instrument was in position and the music burst forth, and simultaneously the banqueters began to march in. They had put off their heavy outside garments but retained their ornaments and insignia. Their white necks and arms gleamed bewitchingly through silvered lace. They moved to their places without the least jostling or awkwardness, their every step and motion proving their high cultivation and grace.

"We must get out of here," whispered Severnius in some consternation. But a squad of servants clogged the doorway and we were crowded backward, and in the interest of self-preservation we took refuge in a small alcove behind a screen of tall hot-house plants with enormous leaves and fronds.

"Good heavens! what shall we do?" cried Severnius, beginning to perspire.

"Let us sit down," said I, who saw nothing very dreadful in the situation except that it was warm, and the odor of the blossoms in front of us was overpowering. There was a bench in the alcove, and we seated ourselves upon it, — I with much comfort, for it was a little cooler down there, and my companion with much fear.

"Would it be a disgrace if we were found here?" I asked.

"I would not be found here for the world!" replied Severnius. "It would not be a disgrace, but it would be considered highly improper. Or, to put it so that you can better understand it, it would be the same as though they were men and we women."

"That is clear!" said I; and I pictured to myself two charming New York girls of my acquaintance secreting themselves in a hall where we City Guards were holding a banquet, — ye gods!

As the feast progressed, and as my senses were almost swept away by the scent of the flowers, I sometimes half fancied that it *was* the City Guards who were seated at the tables.

During the first half-hour everything was carried on with great dignity, speakers being introduced — this occurred in the interim between courses — in proper order, and responding with graceful and well-prepared remarks, which were suitably applauded. But after the glasses had been emptied a time or two all around, there came a change with which I was very familiar. Jokes abounded and jolly little songs were sung, — O, nothing you would take exception to, you know, if they had been men; but women! beautiful, cultivated, charming women, with eyes like stars, with cheeks that matched the dawn, with lips that you would have liked to kiss! And more than this: the preservers of our ideals, the interpreters of our faith, the keepers of our consciences! I felt as though my traditionary idols were shattered, until I remembered that these were not my countrywomen, thank heaven!

Severnius was not at all surprised; he took it all as a matter of course, and was chiefly concerned about how we were going to get out of there. It was more easily accomplished than we could have imagined. The elegant candelabra were a cunningly contrived system of electric lights, and, as sometimes happens with us, they went out suddenly and left the place in darkness for a few convenient seconds. "Quick, now!" cried Severnius with a bound, and there was just time for us to make our escape. We had barely reached the outer door when the whole building was ablaze again.

Severnius offered no comments on the events of the evening, except to say we were lucky to get out as we did, and of course I made none. At my suggestion we stopped at the observatory and spent a few hours there. Lost among the stars, my soul recovered its equilibrium. I have found that little things cease to fret when I can lift my thoughts to great things.

It must have been near morning when I was awakened by the jingling of bells, and a sleigh driving into the *porte cochère.* A few moments later I heard Elodia and her maid coming up the stairs. Her maid attended her everywhere, and stationed herself about like a dummy. She was the sign always that Elodia was not far off; and I am sure she would have laid down her life for her mistress, and would have suffered her tongue to be cut out before she would have betrayed her secrets. I tell you this to show you what a power of fascination Elodia possessed; she seemed a being to be worshiped by high and low.

Severnius and I ate our breakfast alone the following morning. The Supreme Sorceress did not get up, nor did she go down town to attend to business at all during the day. At lunch time she sent her maid down to tell Severnius that she had a headache.

"Quite likely," he returned, as the girl delivered her message; "but I am sorry to hear it. If there is anything I can do for her, tell her to let me know."

The girl made her obeisance and vanished.

"We have to pay for our fun," said Severnius with a sigh.

"I should not think your sister would indulge in such 'fun'!"

I retorted as a kind of relief to my hurt sensibilities, I was so cruelly disappointed in Elodia.

"Why my sister in particular?" returned he with a look of surprise.

"Well, of course, I mean all those women, — why do they do such things? It is unwomanly, it — it is disgraceful!"

I could not keep the word back, and for the first time I saw a flash of anger in my friend's eyes.

"Come," said he, "you must not talk like that! That term may have a different signification to you, but with us it means an insult."

I quickly begged his pardon and tried to explain to him.

"Our women," I said, "never do things of that sort, as I have told you. They have no taste for them and no inclination in that direction, — it is against their very nature. And if you will forgive me for saying so, I cannot but think that such indulgence as we witnessed last night must coarsen a woman's spiritual fibre, and dull the fine moral sense which is so highly developed in her."

"Excuse me," interposed Severnius. "You have shown me in the case of your own sex that human nature is the same on the Earth that it is on Mars. You would not have me think that there are two varieties of human nature on your planet, corresponding with the sexes, would you? You say 'woman's' spiritual fibre and fine moral sense, as though she had an exclusive title to those qualities. My dear sir, it is impossible! you are all born of woman and are one flesh and one blood, whether you are male or female. I admit all you say about the unwholesome influence of such indulgence as wine drinking, late hours, questionable stories and songs, — a night's debauch, in fact, which it requires days sometimes to recover from, — but I must apply it to men as well as women; neither are at their best under such conditions. I think," he went on, "that I begin to understand the distinction which you have curiously mistaken for a radical difference. Your women, you say, have always been in a state of semi-subjection—"

"No, no," I cried, "I never said so! On the contrary, they hold the very highest place with us; they are honored with chivalrous devotion, cared for with the tenderest consideration. We men are their slaves, in reality, though they call us their lords; we work for them, endure hardships for them, give them all that we can of wealth, luxury, ease. And we defend them from danger and save them every annoyance in our power. They are the queens of our hearts and homes."

"That may all be," he replied coolly, "but you admit that they have always been denied their political rights, and it follows that their social rights should be similarly limited. Long abstinence from the indulgences which you regard as purely masculine, has resulted in a habit merely, not a change in their nature."

"Then thank heaven for their abstinence!" I exclaimed.

"That is all very well," he persisted, "but you must concede that in the first place it was forced upon them, and that was an injustice, because they were intelligent beings and your equals."

"They ought to thank us for the injustice, then," I retorted.

"I beg your pardon! they ought not. No doubt they are very lovely and innocent beings, and that your world is the better for them. But they, being restricted in other ways by man's author-ity, or his wishes, or by fear of his disfavor perhaps, have acquired these gentle qualities at the expense of—or in the place of—others more essential to the foundation of character; I mean strength, dignity, self-respect, and that which you once attrib-uted to my sister,—responsibility."

I was bursting with indignant things which I longed to say,

but my position was delicate, and I bit my tongue and was silent.

I will tell you one thing, my heart warmed toward my gentle countrywomen! With all their follies and frivolities, with all their inconsistencies and unaccountable ways, their whimsical fancies and petty tempers, their emotions and their susceptibility to new isms and religions, they still represented my highest and best ideals. And I thought of Elodia, sick upstairs from her last night's carousal, with contempt.

# CHAPTER 4.

## ELODIA.

"If to her lot some female errors fall,
Look to her face and you'll forget them all."—POPE.

My contempt for Elodia vanished at the first intimation of her presence. I had expected to meet her with an air of cold superiority, but when she entered the dining-room that evening with her usual careless aplomb, the glance with which she favored me reduced me to my customary attitude toward her,—that of unquestioning admiration. Our physical nature is weak, and this woman dominated my senses completely, with her beauty, with her melodious voice, her singular magnetic attraction, and every casual expression of her face.

On that particular evening, her dress was more than ordinarily becoming, I thought. She had left off some of the draperies she usually wore about her shoulders, and her round, perfect waist was more fully disclosed in outline. She was somewhat pale, and her eyes seemed larger and darker than their wont, and had deeper shadows. And a certain air of languor that hung about her was an added grace. She had, however, recovered sufficiently from the dissipations of the day before to make herself uncommonly agreeable, and I never felt in a greater degree the charm and stimulus of her presence and conversation.

After dinner she preceded us into the parlor, — which was unusual, for she was always too sparing of her society, and the most we saw of her was at dinner or luncheon time, — and crossed over to an alcove where stood a large and costly harp whose strings she knew well how to thrum.

"Elodia, you have never sung for our friend," said Severnius.

She shook her head, and letting her eyes rest upon me half-unconsciously—almost as if I were not there in fact, for she had a peculiar way of looking at you without actually seeing you, — she went on picking out the air she had started to play. I subjoined a beseeching look to her brother's suggestive remark, but was not sure she noted it. But presently she began to sing and I dropped into a chair and sat spell-bound. Her voice was sweet, with a quality that stirred unwonted feelings; but it was not that alone. As she stood there in the majesty of her gracious womanhood, her exquisite figure showing at its best, her eyes uplifted and a something that meant power radiating from her whole being, I felt that, do what she might, she was still the grandest creature in that world to me!

Soon after she had finished her song, while I was still in the thrall of it, a servant entered the room with a packet for Severnius, who opened and read it with evident surprise and delight.

"Elodia!" he cried, "those friends of mine, those Caskians from Lunismar, are coming to make us a visit."

"Indeed!" she answered, without much enthusiasm, and Severnius turned to me.

"It is on your account, my friend, that I am to be indebted to them for this great pleasure," he explained.

"On my account?" said I.

"Yes, they have heard about you, and are extremely anxious to make your acquaintance?"

"They must be," said Elodia, "to care to travel a thousand miles or so in order to do it."

"Who are they, pray?" I asked.

"They are a people so extraordinarily good," she said with a laugh, "so refined and sublimated, that they cast no shadow in the sun."

Severnius gave her a look of mild protest.

"They are a race exactly like ourselves, outwardly," he said, "who inhabit a mountainous and very picturesque country called Caskia, in the northern part of this continent."

"O, that is where the Perfect Pair came from," I rejoined, remembering what he had told me about Man's origin on Mars.

Elodia smiled. "Has Severnius been entertaining you with our religious fables?" she asked. I glanced at him and saw that he had not heard, he was finishing his letter.

"You will be interested in these Caskians," he said to me animatedly as he folded it up; "I was. I spent some months in Lunismar, their capital, once, studying. They have rare facilities for reading the heavens there, — I mean of their own contrivance, — beside their natural advantages; their high altitude and the clearness of the air."

"And they name themselves after the planetoids and other heavenly bodies," interjected Elodia, "because they live so near the stars. What is the name of the superlative creature you were so charmed with, Severnius?"

"I suppose you mean my friend Calypso's wife, Clytia," returned he.

"O, yes, I remember, — Clytia. Is she to favor us?"

"Yes, and her husband and several others."

"Any other women?"

"One or two, I think."

"And how are we to conduct ourselves during the visitation?"

"As we always do; you will not find that they will put any constraint upon you."

"No, hardly," said Elodia, with a slight curl of the lip.

I was eager to hear more about these singular people,—the more eager, perhaps, because the thought of them seemed to arouse Elodia to an unwonted degree of feeling and interest. Her eyes glowed intensely, and the color flamed brightly in her cheeks.

I pressed a question or two upon Severnius, and he responded:

"According to the traditions and annals of the Caskians, they began many thousands of years ago to train themselves toward the highest culture and most perfect development of which mankind is capable. Their aim was nothing short of the Ideal, and they believed that the ideal was possible. It took many centuries to counteract and finally to eradicate hereditary evils, but their courage and perseverance did not give way, and they triumphed. They have dropped the baser natural propensities—"

"As, in the course of evolution, it is said, certain species of animals dropped their tails to become Man," interupted Elodia.

She rose from the divan on which she had gracefully disposed herself when she ceased playing, and glided from the room, sweeping a bow to us as she vanished, before Severnius or I could interpose an objection to her leaving us. Although there was never any appearance of haste in her manner, she had a swift celerity of movement which made it impossible to anticipate her intention.

Severnius, however, did not care to interpose an objection, I think. He felt somewhat hurt by her sarcastic comments upon his friends, and he expanded more after she had gone.

"You must certainly visit Lunismar before you leave Mars,"

he said. "You will feel well repaid for the trouble. It is a beautiful city, wonderful in its cleanness, in its dearth of poverty and squalor, and in the purity and elevation of its social tone. I think you will wish you might live there always."

There seemed to be a regret in his voice, and I asked:

"Why did not you remain there?"

"Because of my sister," he answered.

"But she will marry, doubtless." For some occult reason I hung upon his reply to this. He shook his head.

"I do not think she will," he said. "And she and I are all that are left of our family."

"She does not like, — or she does not believe in these Caskians?" I hoped he would contradict me, and he did. I had come to found my judgments of people and of things upon Elodia's, even against the testimony of my reason. If she disapproved of her brother's extraordinary friends and thought them an impossible people, why, then, I knew I should have misgivings of them, too; and I wanted to believe in them, not only on Severnius' account, but because they presented a curious study in psychology.

"O, yes, she does," he said. "She thinks that their principles and their lives are all right for themselves, but would not be for her — or for us; and our adoption of them would be simply apish. She is genuine, and she detests imitation. She accepts herself — as she puts it — as she found herself. God, who made all things, created her upon a certain plane of life, and with certain tastes, faculties, passions and propensities, and that it is not her office to disturb or distort the order of His economy."

"She does not argue thus in earnest," I deprecated.

"It is difficult to tell when Elodia is in earnest," he replied. "She thinks my sanctuary in the top story of the house here, is a kind of weakness, because I brought the idea from Lunismar."

"O, then, it is not common here in Thursia for people to have things of that sort in their homes!" I said in surprise.

"Yes, it has gotten to be rather common," he replied.

"Since you put in yours?"

He admitted that to be the case.

"You must think that you have done your country a great good," I began enthusiastically, "in introducing so beautiful an innovation, and —"

"You are mistaken," he interrupted, "I think the contrary; because our rich people, and some who are not rich but only ambitious, took it up as a fad, and I believe it has really worked evil. It is considered aristocratic to have one's own private shrine, and not to go to church at all except in condescension, to patronize the masses. Elodia saw clearly just how it would be, before I began to carry out my plan. She has a logical mind, and her thought travels from one sequence to the next with unfailing accuracy. I recall her saying that one cannot superinduce the customs and habits of one society upon another of a different order, without affectation; and that you cannot put on a new religion, like a new garment, and feel yourself free in it."

"Does she not believe, then, in progress, development?"

"Only along the familiar lines. She thinks you can reach outward and upward from your natural environment, but you must not tear yourself out of it with violence. However, she admitted that my sanctuary was well enough for me, because of my having lived among the Caskians and studied their sublime ethics until I grew into the meanings of them. But no person can take them second-hand from me, because I could not bring away with me the inexpressible something which holds those people together in a perfect Unit. I can go to Caskia and catch the spirit of their religion, but I cannot bring Caskia here. It was a mistake in so far as my neighbors are concerned, since they only see in it, as I have said, a new fashion, a new diversion for their ennuied thoughts."

"What is there peculiar about the religion of those people?" I asked.

"The most peculiar thing about it is that they live it, rather than profess it," he replied.

"I don't think I understand," said I, and after a moment's consideration of the matter in his own mind, he tried to make his meaning clear to me.

"Do you often hear an upright man professing his honesty? It is a part of himself. He is so free of the law which enjoins honesty that he never gives it a thought. So with the man who is truly religious, he had flung off the harness and no longer needs to guide himself by bit and rein, or measure his conduct by the written code. My friends, the Caskians, have emancipated themselves from the thraldom of the law by absorbing its principles into themselves. It was like seed sown in the ground, the germs burst from the husk and shot upward; they are enjoying the flower and the fruit. That which all nations and peoples, and all individuals, prize and desire above everything else in life, is liberty. But I have seen few here in Paleveria who have any conception of the vast spiritual meanings of the word. We limit it to the physical; we say 'personal' liberty, as though that were all. You admire the man of high courage, because in that one thing he is free. So with all the virtues, named and unnamable; he is greatest who has loosed himself the most, who weighs anchor and sails away triumphant and free. But this is but a general picture of the Caskians; let me particularize: we are forbidden to steal, by both our civil and religious canons, — the coarseness of such a command would offend them as much as a direct charge of theft would offend you or myself, so exquisite is their sense of the rights of others, not only in the matter of property but in a thousand subtle ways. Robbery in any form is impossible with them. They would think it a crying sin for one to take the slightest advantage of another, — nay, to neglect an opportunity to assist another in the accomplishment of his rightful purpose would be criminal. We, here on Mars, and you upon the Earth, have discovered very sensitive elements in nature; they have discovered the same in their own souls. Their perceptions are singularly acute, their touch upon each other's lives finely delicate. In this respect we compare with them as the rude blacksmith compares with the worker in precious metals."

"But do they also concern themselves with science?" I asked.

"Assuredly," he answered. "Their inventions are remarkable, their methods infinitely superior to ours. They believe in the triple nature, — the spiritual, the intellectual, and the physical, — and take equal pains in the development and culture of all."

"How wonderful!" I said, remembering that upon the Earth we have waves of culture breaking over the land from time to time, spasmodic, and never the same; today it may be physical, tomorrow intellectual, and by-and-by a superfine spiritual bloom. But, whichever it is, it sacrifices the other two and makes itself supreme.

Severnius went on. As he proceeded, I was struck by the fact that the principles of our Christian civilization formed the basis of Paleverian law.

"I wanted to give you some other instances," he said, "of the 'peculiarities' of the Caskians, as we started out with calling them. There is a law with us against bearing false witness; they hold each other in such honor and in such tenderness, that the command is an idle breath. There is nothing mawkish or sentimental about this, however; they, in fact, make no virtue of it, any more than you or I make a virtue of the things we do habitually—perhaps from unanalyzed motives of policy. You would not strike a man if you knew he would hit back and hurt you worse than he himself was hurt; well, these people have sensibilities so finely developed, that a wrong done to another reacts upon themselves with exquisite suffering. The law and its penalties are both unseen forces, operating on an internal not an external plane. With us, the authority which declares, 'Thou shalt not commit adultery,' becomes powerless at the threshold of marriage. Like other such laws which hold us together in an outward appearance of decency and good order, it is a dead letter to them up to the point where we drop and trample upon it; here they take it up and carry it into their inmost lives and thoughts in a way almost too fine for us to comprehend. Because we have never so much as dreamed of catching the spirit of that law."

"What do you mean?" I demanded, with a wide stare.

"Why, that marriage does not sanction lust. The Caskians hold that the exercise of the procreative faculty is a divine function, and should never be debased to mere animal indulgence. It has been said upon Divine Authority—as we believe—that if a man look upon a woman to lust after her, he has committed adultery in his heart. The Caskians interpret that to mean a man's wife, the same as any other woman, because—they hold—one who owes his being to lust and passion naturally inherits the evil and the curse, just as surely as though wedlock had not concealed the crime. Their children are conceived in immaculate purity."

My look of prolonged amazement called out the question:

"Have you no such class in any of your highly civilized countries?"

"No, I think not. With us, children do not come in answer

to an intelligent desire for their existence, but are too often simply the result of indulgence, and so unwelcome that their prenatal life is overshadowed by sorrow and crime."

"Well," said he, "it is the same here; our people believe that conception without lust is an impossibility in nature, and that instances of it are supernatural. And certainly it is incredible unless your mind can grasp the problem, or rather the great fact, of a people engaged for centuries in eliminating the purely animal instincts from their consciousness."

After a moment he added:

"In Caskia it would be considered shocking if a pair contemplating marriage were to provide themselves with only one suite of rooms, to be shared together day and night. Even the humblest people have their respective apartments; they think such separateness is absolutely essential to the perfect development of the individual, — for in the main we each must stand alone, — and to the preservation of moral dignity, and the fine sentiment and mutual respect which are almost certain to be lost in the lawlessness of undue familiarity. The relation between my friend Calypso and his wife is the finest thing I ever saw; they are lovers on the highest plane. It would be an impossibility for either of them to say or do a coarse or improper thing in the other's presence, or to presume, in any of the innumerable ways you and I are familiar with in our observations of husbands and wives, upon the marriage bond existing between them. This matter of animal passion," he went on, after a little pause, "has been at the bottom of untold crimes, and unnumbered miseries, in our land. I doubt if any other one thing has been prolific of more or greater evils, — even the greed of wealth. Men, and women, too, have sacrificed kingdoms for it, have bartered their souls for it. Countless homes have been desolated because of it, countless lives and hearts have been laid on its guilty altar. We ostracize the bastard; he is no more impure than the offspring of legalized licentiousness, and the law which protects the one and despises the other, cannot discriminate in the matter of after effects, cannot annul or enforce the curse of heredity. With these people the law of chastity is graven in the inmost heart, and in this matter, as in all others, each generation acknowledges its obligation to the next."

# CHAPTER 5.

## THE VAPORIZER.

"Portable ecstasies . . . corked up in a pint bottle."—DE QUINCEY.

I was glad when spring came, when the trees began to bud, the grass to grow, the flowers to bloom; for, of all the seasons, I like it best,—this wonderful resurrection of life and sweetness!

Thursia is a fine city,—not only in its costly and architecturally and aesthetically perfect buildings, public and private, but in its shaded avenues, its parks, lawns, gardens, fountains, its idyllic statues, and its monuments to greatness.

Severnius took pains to exhibit all its attractions to me, driving with me slowly through the beautiful streets, and pointing out one conspicuous feature and another. Of course there were some streets which were not beautiful, but he avoided those as much as possible,—as I have done myself when I have had friends visiting me in New York. It is a compliment to your guest to show him the best there is and to spare him the worst.

But often, too, we took long walks through fields and woods. When Elodia accompanied us, which she did a few times, the whole face of nature smiled, and I thought Paleveria the most incomparably charming country I had ever seen. Her presence gave importance to everything, — the song of a bird, the opening of a humble little flower, the babbling of water. But other things absorbed most of her time, — we only got the scraps, the remnants. When she was with us she relaxed, as though we were in some sort a recreation. She amused herself with us just as I have seen a busy father amuse himself with his family for an hour or so of an evening. And I think we really planned our little theatricals of evening conversation for her, — at least I did. I saved up whatever came to me of thought or incident to give to her at the dinner table. And she appreciated it; her mind bristled with keen points, upon which any ideas let loose were caught in a flash. The sudden illumination of her countenance when a new thing, or even an old thing in a new dress, was presented to her, was of such value to me that I found myself laying traps for it, inventing stories and incidents to touch her fancy.

Besides her banking interests, over which she kept a close surveillance, she had a great many other matters that required to be looked after. As soon as the weather was fine enough, and business activities in the city began to be redoubled, especially in the matter of real estate, she made a point of driving about by herself to inspect one piece of property and another, and to make plans and see that they were carried out according to her ideas. And she was just as conscientious in the discharge of her official duties. She was constantly devising means for the betterment of the schools, both as to buildings and methods of instruction. I believe she knew every teacher personally, — and there must have been several thousand, — and her relations with all of them were cordial and friendly. Her approbation was a thing they strove for and valued, — not because of her official position and the authority she held in her hands, but because of a power which was innate in herself and that made her a leader and a protector.

But I was too selfish to yield my small right to her society,—the right only of a guest in her house,—to these greater claims with absolute sweetness and patience.

"Why does she take all these things upon herself?" I asked of Severnius.

"Because she has a taste for them," he replied. "Or, as she would say, a need of them. It is an internal hunger. It is her nature to exert herself in these ways."

"I cannot believe it is her nature; it is no woman's nature," I retorted. "It is a habit which she has cultivated until it has got the mastery of her."

"Perhaps," returned Severnius, who was never much disposed to argue about his sister's vagaries—as they seemed to me.

"All this is mannish," I went on. "There are other things for women to do. Why does she not give her time and attention to the softer graces, to feminine occupations?"

"I see," he laughed; "you want her to drop these weighty matters and devote herself to amusing us! and you call that 'feminine.'"

I joined in his laugh ruefully.

"Perhaps I am narrow, and selfish, too," I admitted; "but she is so charming, she brings so much into our conversations whenever we can entice her to spend a moment with us."

"Yes, that is true," he answered. "She gleans her ideas from a large and varied field."

"I do not mean her ideas, so much as—well, as the delicious flavor of her presence and personality."

"Her presence and her personality would not have much flavor, my friend, if she had no ideas, I am thinking."

"O, yes, they would," I insisted. "They are the ether in which our own thoughts expand and take shape and color. They are the essence of her supreme beauty."

He shook his head. "Beauty is nothing without intelligence. What is the camellia beside the rose? Elodia is the rose. She has several pleasing qualities that appeal to you at one and the same time."

This was rather pretty, but a man's praises of his sister always sound tame to me. "She is adorable!" I cried with fervor. We were walking toward a depot connected with a great railway. For the first time I was to try the speed of a Marsian train. Severnius wanted me to visit the city of Frambesco, some two hundred miles from Thursia, in another state.

After a short, ruminating silence I broke out again:

"We don't even have her company evenings, to any extent. What does she do with her evenings?"

"Who? O, Elodia! Why, she goes to her club. For recreation, you know."

"That is complimentary to you and me," I said coolly.

He brought his spectacles to bear upon me somewhat sharply.

"Don't you think you are a little unreasonable?" he demanded. "You have curious ideas about individual liberty! Now, we hold that every soul shall be absolutely free, — that is, in its relations to other souls; it shall not be coerced by any other. It is as though souls were stars suspended in space, each moving in its appointed orbit. No one has the right to disturb the poise and equilibrium of another, not even the one nearest it. That is a Caskian idea, by the way; about the only one Elodia is enamored of. These souls, or spheres, are extremely sensitive; and they may, and do, exert a tremendous influence, one upon another, — but without violence."

"Your meaning is clear," I said coldly. "My powers of attraction in this case are feeble. Is the club you speak of composed entirely of women?"

"Certainly."

"Do not the men here have clubs?"

"O, yes; I belong to one, though I do not often attend. I will take you to visit it, — I wonder I had not thought of it before! But those things are disturbing; we scientists like to keep our minds clear, like the lenses of our telescopes."

"Is Elodia's club a literary one!" I asked, though I was almost sure it was not.

"O, no; it is for recreation purely, as I said. The same kind of a club, I suppose, that you men have. Of course, they have the current literature, which they skim over and discuss, so as to keep themselves informed about what is going on in the world. It is the only way you can keep up with the times, I think, for no one can read everything. They have games and various diversions. Elodia's clubhouse is furnished with elegant baths, for women have an extraordinary fondness for bathing. And they have a gymnasium, — you notice what splendid figures most of our women have! — and of course a wine cellar."

"Severnius!" I cried. "You don't mean to tell me that these women have wines in their clubhouse?"

"Why, yes," said he.

"And it is tolerated, allowed, nobody objects?"

"O, yes, there are plenty of objectors," he replied. "There is a very strong anti-intoxicant element here, but it has no actual force and exerts but little influence in — in our circles."

Severnius was too modest a man to boast of belonging to the upper class of society, but that was what "our circles" meant.

"But do not the male relatives of these women object, — their husbands, fathers, brothers?"

"No, indeed, why should they? We do the same things they do, without demur from them."

"But they should be looking after their domestic affairs, their children, their homes."

"My dear sir! they have servants to attend to those matters."

It seemed useless to discuss these things with Severnius, his point of view concerning the woman question was so different from mine. Nevertheless, I persisted.

"Tell me, Severnius, do women on this planet do everything that men do?"

"They have that liberty," he replied, "but there is sometimes a difference of tastes."

"I am glad to hear it!"

"For instance, they do not smoke. By the way, have a cigar?" He passed me his case and we both fired up. There is a peculiarly delightful flavor in Marsian tobacco.

"They have a substitute though," he added, removing the fragrant weed from his lips to explain. "They vaporize."

"They what?"

"They have a small cup, a little larger than a common tobacco pipe, which they fill with alcohol and pulverized valerian root. This mixture when lighted diffuses a kind of vapor, a portion of which they inhale through the cup-stem, a slender, tortuous tube attached to the cup. The most of it, however, goes into the general air."

"Good heavens!" I cried, "valerian! the most infernal, diabolical smell that was ever emitted from any known or unknown substance."

"It is said to be soothing to the nerves," he replied.

"But do you not find it horribly disagreeable, unbearable?" I suddenly recollected that, in passing through the upper hall of the house, I had once or twice detected this nauseating odor, in the neighborhood of Elodia's suite of rooms.

"Yes, I do," he answered, "when I happen to come in contact with it, which is seldom. They are careful not to offend others to whom the vapor is unpleasant. Elodia is very delicate in these matters; she is fond of the vapor habit, but she allows no suggestion of it to cling to her garments or vitiate her breath."

"It must be a great care to deodorize herself," I returned, with ill-concealed contempt.

"That is her maid's business," said he.

"It is not injurious to health?" I asked.

"Quite so; it often induces frightful diseases, and is sometimes fatal to life even.

"And yet they persist in it! I should think you would interfere in your sister's case."

"Well," said he, "the evils which attend it are really no greater than those that wait upon the tobacco habit; and, as I smoke, I can't advise with a very good grace. I have a sort of blind faith that these good cigars of mine are not going to do me any harm, — though I know they have harmed others; and I suppose Elodia reasons in the same friendly way with her vapor cup."

The train stood on the track ready to start. I was about to spring up the steps of the last car when Severnius stopped me.

"Not that one," he said; "that is the woman's special."

I stepped back, and read the word *Vaporizer*, — printed in large gilt letters, — bent like a bow on the side of the car.

"Do you mean to tell me, Severnius," I exclaimed, "that the railroad company devotes one of these magnificent coaches exclusively to the use of persons addicted to the obnoxious habit we have been speaking of?"

"That is about the size of it," he returned, — he borrowed the phrase from me. "Come, make haste, or we shall be left; the next car is the smoker; we'll step into that and finish these cigars, after which I'll show you what sumptuous parlor coaches we have."

As we mounted to the platform I could not resist glancing into the *Vaporizer*. There were only two or three ladies there, and one of them held in her ungloved hand the little cup with the tortuous stem which my friend had described to me. From it there issued a pale blue smoke or vapor, and oh! the smell of it! I held my breath and hurried after Severnius.

"That is the most outrageous, abominable thing I ever heard of!" I declared, as we entered the smoker and took our seats.

"O, it is nothing," he returned, smiling; "you are a very fastidious fellow. I saw you look into that car; did you observe the lady in blue?"

"I should think I did! she was in the act," I replied. "And I recognized her, too; she is that Madam Claris you introduced me to in the Auroras' Temple, is she not?"

"Yes; but did you notice her cup?"

"Not particularly."

"It is carved out of the rarest wood we have,—wood that hardens like stone with age,—and has an indestructible lining and is studded with costly gems; the thing is celebrated, an heirloom in Claris' family. They like to sport those things, the owners of them do. They are a mark of distinction,—or, as they might say in some of your countries, a patent of nobility."

"I suppose, then, that only the rich and the aristocratic 'vaporize'?"

"By no means; whatever the aristocracy do, humble folk essay to imitate. These vapor cups are made in great quantities, of the commonest clay, and sold for a penny apiece."

"Then it must be a natural taste, among your women?" said I.

"No, no more than smoking is among men. They say it is nauseating in the extreme, at first, and requires great courage and persistence to continue in it up to the point of liking. There is no doubt that it becomes very agreeable to them in the end, and that it is almost impossible to break the habit when once it is fixed."

"And what do they do with their cups, — I mean, how do they carry them about when they are not using them?" I asked.

"Put them in a morocco case, the same as you would a meerschaum, and drop them into a fanciful little bag which they wear on the arm, suspended by a chain or ribbon."

Frambesco could not compare with Thursia either in size or beauty; and it had a totally different air, a kind of swagger, you might say. I felt the mercury in my moral barometer drop down several degrees as we walked about the streets amid much filth, and foul odors, and unsightly spectacles.

I made the natural comments to my friend, and he replied that neither Frambesco nor any other city on the continent could hold a candle to Thursia, where the best of every thing was centered.

We observed a great many enormous placards posted about conspicuously, announcing a game of fisticuffs to take place that afternoon in an amphitheatre devoted to such purposes; and we decided to look in upon it. I think it was I who suggested it, for I had no little curiosity about the "tactics" of the manly art in that country, having seen Sullivan and several other famous hitters in our own.

Severnius had considerable difficulty in procuring tickets, and finally paid a fabulous price to a speculator for convenient seats. The great cost of admission of course kept out the rabble, and, in a way, it was an eminently respectable throng that was assembled, — I mean in so far as money and rich clothes make for respectability. But there was an unmistakable coarseness in most of the faces, or if not that, a curiosity which bordered on coarseness. I was amazed to see women in the audience; but this was nothing to the horror that quivered through me like a deadly wound, when the combatants sprang into the arena and squared off for action. For they, too, were women, — women with tender, rosy flesh; with splendid dark eyes gleaming with high excitement. Their long, fair hair was braided and twisted into a hard knot on top of the head. They wore no gloves. Ah, a woman's hands are soft enough without padding! — I thought.

They went at it in scientific fashion and were careful to observe the etiquette of the game; it was held "foul" to attack the face. In fact it was more of a wrestling than a sparring match, — a test of strength, prowess, agility. But I recoiled from it with loathing, and feeling myself grow sick and faint, I muttered something to Severnius and rushed out of the place. He followed me, of course; the performance was quite as distasteful to him as to me, the only difference being that he was familiar with the idea and I was not.

As I passed out, I observed that many of the women were vaporizing and many of the men smoking. I suppose it was, in part, the intolerable abomination of these commingled smells that affected me, for I experienced a physical as well as moral nausea. I did not get over it for hours, and I was as glad as a child when it came time to take the train back to Thursia.

My disgust was so great that I could not discuss the matter with Severnius, as I was wont to discuss other matters with him. There was one thing for which I was supremely thankful, — that Elodia was not there.

A few days later, the subject accidentally came up, and I had the satisfaction of hearing her denounce the barbarity as emphatically as I could denounce it, — and more sweepingly, for she included male fighters in her condemnation, and I was unable to make her see that that was quite another matter.

# CHAPTER 6.

CUPID'S GARDENS.

"O, in what sweets dost thou thy sins enclose."—SHAKESPEARE.

During the time that intervened before the arrival of the Caskians, to make their proposed visit, I gleaned many more interesting hints from Severnius relative to their life and conduct, which greatly whetted my curiosity to meet them. For instance, we were one day engaged in a conversation, he, Elodia, and myself, upon the subject of the province of poetry in history,—but that does not matter,—when dinner was announced in the usual way; that is, the way which assumes without doubt that nothing else in the world is so important as dinner. It may be a bell, or a gong, or a verbal call, but it is as imperative as the command of an autocrat. It brings to the ground, with the suddenness of a mental shock, the finest flights of the imagination. It wakes the soul from transcendent dreams, cools the fervor of burning eloquence, breaks the spell of music. More than this: it destroys the delicate combination of mental states and forces sometimes induced when several highly trained minds have fallen into an attitude of acute sympathy toward one another,—a rare and ineffable thing!—and are borne aloft through mutual helpfulness to regions of thought and emotion infinitely exalted, which can never be reproduced.

I have often had this experience myself, and have wished that the cook was a creature of supernatural intuitions, so that he could divine the right moment in which to proclaim that the soup was served! There is a right moment, a happy moment, when the flock of intellectual birds, let loose to whirl and circle and soar in the upper air, descend gracefully and of their own accord to the agreeable level of soup.

On the occasion to which I have referred, I tried to ignore, and to make my companions ignore, the discordant summons—by a kind of dominant action of my mind upon theirs—in order that we might continue the talk a little longer. We three had never before shown ourselves off to each other to such striking advantage; we traveled miles in moments, we expanded, we unrolled reams of intelligence which were apprehended in a flash, as a whole landscape is apprehended in a glare of lightning. It was as if our words were tipped with flame and carried their illumination along with them. I knew that there never would, never could, come another such time, but Elodia thwarted my effort to hold it a moment longer.

"Come!" she cried gayly, rising to her feet and breaking off in the middle of a beautiful sentence, the conclusion of which I was waiting for with tremors of delight,—for her views, as it happened, accorded with mine,—"the ideal may rule in art, but not in life; it is very unideal to eat, but the stomach is the dial of the world."

"We make it so," said Severnius.

"Of course, we make all our sovereigns," she returned. "We set the dial to point at certain hours, and it simply holds us to our agreement,—it and the *chef.*"

"That reminds me of our Caskian friends," said Severnius. "They have exceedingly well-ordered homes, but occasionally one of the three Natures waits upon another; the Mind may yield to some contingency connected with the Body, or the Body waive its right in favor of the Spirit."

"I had supposed they were more machine-like," commented Elodia, with her usual air of not being able to take a great interest in the Caskians.

"They are the farthest from that of any people I know," he answered. "They have great moments, now and then, when a few people are gathered together, and their thought becomes electrical and their minds mingle as you have seen the glances of eyes mingle in a language more eloquent than speech,—and, to tell the truth, we ourselves have such moments, I'll not deny that; but the difference is, that they appreciate the value of them and hold them fast, while we open our hands and let them fly away like uncoveted birds, or worthless butterflies. I have actually known a meal to be dropped out entirely in Calypso's house, forgotten in the felicity of an intellectual or spiritual delectation!"

"Thank heaven, that we live in Thursia!" cried Elodia, "where such lapses are impossible."

"They are next to impossible there," said Severnius; "But they do happen, which proves a great deal. They are in the nature of miracles, they are so wonderful,—and yet not so wonderful. We forget sometimes that we have a soul, and they forget that they have a body; there's no great difference."

"There is a mighty difference," answered Elodia. "We are put into a material world, to enjoy material benefits. I should think those people would miss a great deal of the actual good of life in the pursuit of the unactual,—always taking their flights from lofty pinnacles, and skipping the treasures that lie in the valleys."

"On the contrary," he returned, "the humblest little flower that grows, the tiniest pebble they pick up on the beach, the smallest voice in nature, all have place in their economy. They miss nothing; they gather up into their lives all the treasures that nature scatters about. If a bird sings, they listen and say, 'That song is for me;' or, if a blossom opens, 'I will take its beauty into my heart.' These things, which are free to all, they accept freely. Their physical senses are supplemented, — duplicated as it were, in finer quality, — by exquisite inner perceptions."

The morning after this conversation, Severnius and I took a long drive in a new direction. We went up the river a mile or so, the road winding through an avenue of century-old elms, whose great, graceful branches interlocked overhead and made a shade so dense that the very atmosphere seemed green. We were so earnestly engaged in conversation that I did not observe when we left the avenue and entered a wood. We drove some distance through this, and then the road branched off and skirted round a magnificent park, — the finest I had seen, — bordered by a thick hedge, all abloom with white, fragrant flowers and fenced with a fretwork of iron, finished with an inverted fringe of bristling points. Within, were evidences of costly and elaborate care; the trees were of noble growth and the greensward like stretches of velvet over which leaf-shadows flickered and played. The disposition of shrubbery and flowers, the chaste and beautiful statuary, the fountains, brooklets, arbors, and retreats; the rustic efforts in bridges, caves, grottoes, and several graceful arches, hidden in wreathed emerald, from which snow-white cherubs with wings on their shoulders peeped roguishly, all betokened ingenious design, and skilful and artistic execution.

Beyond, seen vaguely through the waving foliage, were handsome buildings, of the elegant cream-colored stone so much in vogue in Thursia. Here and there, I espied a fawn; one pretty creature, with a ribbon round its neck, was drinking at a fountain, and at the same time some beautiful birds came and perched upon the marble rim and dipped into the sparkling water.

"How lovely! how idyllic!" I cried. "What place is it, Severnius, and why have I never seen it before?"

His answer came a little reluctantly, I thought. "It is called Cupid's Gardens."

"And what does it mean?" I asked.

"Does not its name and those naked imps sufficiently explain it?" he replied. As I looked at him, a blush actually mantled his cheek. "It is a rendezvous," he explained, "where women meet their lovers."

"How curious! I never heard of such a thing," said I. "Do you mean that the place was planned for that purpose, or did the name get fastened upon it through accident? Surely you are joking, Severnius; women can receive their lovers in their homes here, the same as with us!"

"Their suitors, not their lovers," he replied.

"You make a curious distinction!" said I.

"Women sometimes marry their suitors, never their lovers, — any more than men marry their mistresses."

"Great heavens, Severnius!" I felt the blood rush to my face and then recede, and a cold perspiration broke out all over me. There was a question in my mind which I did not dare to ask, but Severnius divined it.

"Is it a new idea to you?" said he. "Have you no houses of prostitution in your country, licensed by law, as this is?"

"For men, not for women," said I.

"Ah! another of your peculiar discriminations!" he returned.

"Well, surely you will agree with me that in this matter, at least, there should be discrimination?" I urged.

He shook his head with that exasperating stubbornness one occasionally finds in sweet-tempered people.

"No, I cannot agree with you, even in this," he replied. "What possible reason is there why men, more than women, should be privileged to indulge in vice?"

"Why, in the very nature of things!" I cried. "There is a hygienic principle involved; you know, — it is a statistical fact, — that single men are neither so vigorous nor so long-lived as married men, and a good many men do not marry."

"Well, a good many more women do not marry; what of those?"

"Severnius! I cannot believe you are in earnest. Women! — that is quite another matter. Women are differently constituted from men; their nature —"

"O, come!" he interrupted; "I thought we had settled that question — that their nature is of a piece with our own. It happens in your world, my friend, that your women were kept to a strict line of conduct, according to your account, by a severe discipline, — including even the death penalty, — until their virtue, from being long and persistently enforced, grew into a habit and finally became a question of honor."

"Yes, stronger than death, thank God!" I affirmed.

"Well, then, it seems to me that the only excuse men have to offer for their lack of chastity—I refer to the men on your planet — is that they have not been hedged about by the wholesome restraints that have developed self-government in women. I cannot admit your 'hygienic' argument in this matter; life is a principle that needs encouragement, and a man of family has more incentives to live, and usually his health is better cared for, than a single man, that is all."

We rode in silence for some time. I finally asked, nodding toward the beautiful enclosure still in view:

"How do they manage about this business; do they practice any secrecy?"

"Of course!" he replied. "I hope you do not think we live in open and shameless lawlessness? Usually it is only the very wealthy who indulge in such 'luxuries,' and they try to seal the lips of servants and go-betweens with gold. But it does not always work; it is in the nature of those things to leak out."

"And if one of these creatures is found out, what then?" I asked.

He answered with some severity:

"'Creatures' is a harsh name to apply to women, some of whom move in our highest circles!"

"I beg your pardon! Call them what you like, but tell me, what happens when there is an *exposé?* Are they denounced, ostracized, sat upon?" I inquired.

"No, not so bad as that," said he. "Of course there is a scandal, but it makes a deal of difference whether the scandal is a famous or an infamous one. If the woman's standing is high in other respects, — if she has money, political influence, talent, attractiveness, — there is very little made of it; or if society feels itself particularly insulted, she may conciliate it by marrying an honest man whose respectability and position protect her."

"What! does an honest man — a gentleman — ever marry such a woman as that?" I cried.

"Frequently; and sometimes they make very good wives. But it is risky. I have a friend, a capital fellow, who was so unfortunate as to attract such a woman, and who finally yielded to her persuasions and married her."

"Heavens! do the women propose?"

"Certainly, when they choose to do so; what is there objectionable in that?"

I made no reply, and he continued, "My friend, as I said, succumbed to her pleadings partly — as I believe — because she threw herself upon his mercy, though she is a beautiful women, and he might have been fascinated to some extent. She told him that his love and protection would be her salvation, and that his denial of her would result in her total ruin; and that for his sake she would reform her life. He is both chivalrous and tender, and, withal, a little romantic, and he consented. My opinion is that, if she could have had him without marriage, she would have preferred it; but he is a true man, a man of honor. Women of her sort like virtuous men, and seldom marry any other. Her love proved to be an ephemeral passion — such as she had had before — and the result has been what you might expect, though Claris is not, by any means, the worst woman in the world."

"Claris?" I exclaimed.

"Ah! I did not mean to speak her name," he returned in some confusion; "and I had forgotten that you knew her. Well, yes, since I have gone so far, it is my friend Massilia's wife that I have been speaking of. In some respects she is an admirable woman, but she has broken her husband's heart and ruined his life."

"Admirable!" I repeated with scorn; "why, in my country, such conduct would damn a woman eternally, no matter what angelic qualities she might possess. She would be shown no quarter in any society — save the very lowest."

"And how about her counterpart of the other sex?" asked Severnius, slyly.

I disregarded this, and returned:

"Did he not get a divorce?"

"No; the law does not grant a divorce in such a case. There was where Claris was shrewder than her husband; she made herself safe by confessing her misdeeds to him, and cajoling him into marrying her in spite of them."

"I beg your pardon, but what a fool he was!"

Severnius acquiesced in this. "I tried to dissuade him," he said, "before the miserable business was consummated, — he made me his confidant, — but it was too late, she had him under her influence."

Another silence fell upon us, which I broke by asking, "Who were those pretty youngsters we saw lounging about on the lawn back there?" I referred to several handsome young men whom I had observed strolling through the beautiful grounds.

He looked at me in evident surprise at the question, and replied:

"Why, those are some of the professional 'lovers.'"

"Great Caesar's ghost!"

"Yes," he went on; "some of our most promising youths are decoyed into those places. It is a distressing business, — a hideous business! And, on the other hand, there are similar institutions where lovely young girls are the victims. I do not know which is the more deplorable, — sometimes I think the latter is. A tender mother would wish that her daughter had never been born, if she should take up with such a life; and an honorable father would rather see his son gibbeted than to find him inside that railing."

"I should think so!" I responded, and inquired, "What kind of standing have these men in the outside world?"

"About the same that a leper would have. They are ignored and despised by the very women who court their caresses here. In fact, they are on a level with the common, paid courtesan, — the lowest rank there is. I have often thought it a curious thing that either men or women should so utterly despise these poor instruments of their sensual delights!"

My friend saw that I was too much shocked to moralize on the subject, and he presently began to explain, and to modify the facts a little.

"You see, these fellows, when they begin this sort of thing, are mostly mere boys, with the down scarcely started on their chins; in the susceptible, impressionable stage, when a woman's honeyed words — ay, her touch, even — may turn the world upside down to them. The life, of course, has its attractions, — money and luxury; to say nothing of the flattery, which is sweeter. Still, few, if any, adopt it deliberately. Often they are wilily drawn into 'entanglements' outside; for the misery of it is, that good society, as I have said before, throws its cloak around these specious beguilers, and the unfortunate dupe does not dream whither he is being led, — youth has such a sincere faith in beauty, and grace, and feminine charm! Sometimes reverses and disaster, of one kind or another, or a cheerless home environment, drive a young man into seeking refuge and lethean pleasures here. It is a form of dissipation similar to the drink habit, only a thousand times worse."

"Worse?" I cried. "It is infernal, diabolical, damnable! And it is woman who accomplishes this horrible ruin! — and is 'received' in society, which, if too flagrantly outraged, will not forgive her unless she marries some good man!"

"O, not always that," protested Severnius; "the unlucky sinner sometimes recovers caste by a course of penitence, by multiplying her subscriptions to charities, and by costly peace-offerings to the aforesaid outraged society."

"What sort of peace-offerings?" I asked.

"Well, an entertainment, perhaps, something superb, something out of the common; or maybe a voyage in her private yacht. Bait of that sort is too tempting for any but the high and mighty, the real aristocrats, to withstand. The simply respectable, but weak-hearted, — who are a little below her level in point of wealth, position, or ancestry, — fall into her net. I have observed that a woman who has forfeited her place in the highest rank of society usually begins her reascent by clutching hold of the skirts of honest folk who are flattered by her condescension, and whose sturdy arms assist her to rise again."

"I have observed the same thing myself," I rejoined, but he had not finished; there was a twinkle in his eye as he went on:

"If you were to reveal the secret of your air-ship to a woman of this kind she would probably seize upon it as a means of salvation; she would have one constructed, on a large and handsome scale, and invite a party to accompany her on an excursion to the Earth. And though she were the worst of her class, every mother's son — and daughter — of us would accept! For none of us hold our self-respect at a higher figure than that, I imagine."

"Yes, Severnius, you do," I replied emphatically.

"I beg your pardon! I would knock off a good deal for a visit to your planet," he said, laughing.

By this time we had left Cupid's Gardens far behind. The road bent in again toward the river, which we presently crossed. If it had not been for the dreadful things I had just listened to, I think I should have been in transports over the serene loveliness of the prospect around us. The view was especially fine from the summit of the bridge; it is a "high" bridge, for the Gyro is navigated by great steam-ships and high-masted schooners.

Severnius bade the driver stop a moment that we might contemplate the scene, but I had little heart for its beauties. And yet I can recall the picture now with extraordinary clearness. The river has many windings, and the woods often hide it from view; but it reappears, again and again, afar off, in green meadows and yellowing fields, — opalescent jewels in gold or emerald setting. Here and there, in the distance, white sails were moving as if on land. Far beyond were vague mountain outlines, and over all, the tender rose-blush of the sky. The sweetness of it, contrasted with the picture newly wrought in my mind, saddened me.

Some distance up the river, on the other side, we passed an old, dilapidated villa, or group of buildings jumbled together without regard to effect evidently, but yet picturesque. They were half hidden in mammoth forest trees that had never been trimmed or trained, but spread their enormous limbs wheresoever they would. Unpruned shrubbery and trailing vines rioted over the uneven lawn, and the rank, windblown grass, too long to stand erect, lay in waves like a woman's hair.

In a general way, the lawn sloped downward toward the road, so that we could see nearly the whole of it over the high, and ugly, board fence which inclosed it. Under the trees, a little way back, I observed a group of young girls lolling in hammocks and idling in rustic chairs. They caught sight of us and sprang up, laughing boisterously. I thought they were going to run away in pretended and playful flight; but instead, they came toward us, and blew kisses at us off their fingers.

I looked at Severnius. "What does this mean?" I asked.

"Why," he said, and the blush mantled his handsome face again, "this place is the counterpart of Cupid's Gardens—a resort for men."

"I thought so," I replied.

By-and-by he remarked, "I hope you will not form too bad an opinion of us, my friend! You have learned to-day what horrible evils exist among us, but I assure you that the sum total of the people who practice them constitutes but a small proportion of our population. And the good people here, the great majority, look upon these things with the same aversion and disgust that you do, and are doing their best—or they think they are—to abolish them."

"How?—by legislation?" I asked.

"Partly; but more through education. Our preachers and teachers have taken the matter up, but they are handicapped by the delicacy of the question and the privacy involved in it, which seems to hinder discussion even, and to forestall advice; though this is the only way to accomplish anything, I think. I have very little faith in legislative measures against secret vices; it is like trying to dam a stream which cannot be dammed but must break out somewhere. I am convinced that my friends, the Caskians, have solved the question in the only possible way—by elevating and purifying the marriage relation. I hope some good may be accomplished by the visit of the few who are coming here!"

"Will they preach or lecture?" I asked, with what seemed to me a moment later to be stupid simplicity.

"O, no!" replied Severnius, with the same air of modest but emphatic protest which they themselves would have doubtless assumed had the question been put to them. "It was simply their personal influence I had reference to. I do not know that I can make you understand, but their presence always seemed to me like a disinfectant of evil. With myself, when I was among them, all the good that was in me responded to their nobility; the evil in me slept, I suppose."

I made a skeptical rejoinder to the implication in his last sentence, for to me he seemed entirely devoid of evil; and we finished the drive in silence.

# CHAPTER 7.

### NEW FRIENDS.

"Having established his equality with class after class, of those
with whom he would live well, he still finds certain others, before
whom he cannot possess himself, because they have somewhat fairer,
somewhat grander, somewhat purer, which extorts homage of him."
— EMERSON.

It is scarcely egotistical for me to say that I was much sought
after, not only by the citizens of Thursia, but by many distinguished people from other cities and countries. Among them
were many men and women of great scientific learning, who made
me feel that I ought to have provided myself with a better equipment of knowledge relative to my own world, before taking my
ambitious journey to Mars! They were exceedingly polite, but
I fear they were much disappointed in many of my hazy responses
to their eager questionings. I learned by this experience the great
value of exact information. In a country like ours, where so much,
and so many sorts, of knowledge are in the air, a person is apt,
unless he is a student of some particular thing, to get little more
than impressions.

There was I, — an average (let me hope!) American citizen, —
at the mercy of inquisitive experts in a hundred different arts

and trades, concerning which, in the main, my ideas might be conservatively described as "general." You may imagine how unsatisfactory this was to people anxious to know about our progress in physics and chemistry, botany, and the great family of "ologies," — or rather about our processes in developing the principles of these great sciences.

With the astronomers and the electricians I got along all right; and I was also able to make myself interesting, — or so I fancied — in describing our social life, our educational and political institutions, and our various forms of religion. Our modes of dress were a matter of great curiosity to most of these people, and I was often asked to exhibit my terrestial garments.

It was when the crowd of outside visitors was at its thickest that the Caskians arrived, and as their stay was brief, covering only two days, you may suppose that we did not advance far on the road to mutual acquaintance. But to tell the truth, there was not a moment's strangeness between us after we had once clasped hands and looked into each other's eyes. It might have been partly due to my own preparedness to meet them with confidence and trust; but more, I think, to their singular freedom from the conventional barriers with which we hedge round our selfness. Their souls spoke to mine, and mine answered back, and the compact of friendship was sealed in a glance.

I cannot hope to give you a very clear idea of their perfect naturalness, their perfect dignity, their kindliness, or their delightful gayety, — before which stiffness, formality, ceremony, were borne down, dissolved as sunshine dissolves frost. No menstruum is so wonderful as the quality of merriment, take it on any plane of life; when it reaches the highest, and is subtilized by cultured and refined intellects, it creates an atmosphere in which the most frigid autocrat of society, and of learning, too, must thaw. The haughtiest dame cannot keep her countenance in the face of this playful spirit toying with her frills. The veriest old dry-as-dust, hibernating in mouldy archaeological chambers, cannot resist the blithesome thought which dares to illumine his antique treasures with a touch of mirth.

I was struck by Clytia's beauty, which in some ways seemed finer than Elodia's. The two women were about the same height and figure. But Clytia's coloring was pure white and black, except for the healthy carmine of her lips, and occasional fluctuations of the rose tint in her cheeks.

I was present when they first met, in the drawing-room. Elodia rose to her full stature, armed cap-a-pie with her stateliest manner, but with a gracious sense of hospitality upon her. I marked with pleasure that Clytia did not rush upon her with any exuberance of gladness, — as some women would have done in a first meeting with their friend's sister, — for that would have disgusted Elodia and driven her to still higher ground. How curious are our mental attitudes toward our associates, and how quickly adjusted! Here had I been in Elodia's house, enjoying her companionship — if not her friendship — for months; and yet, you see, I secretly did not wish any advantage to be on her side. It could not have been disloyalty, for the impulse was swift and involuntary. I would like to suppose that it sprang from my instantaneous recognition of the higher nature; but it did not. It was due, no doubt, to a fear for the more timid one — as I fancied it to be. I had a momentary sensation as of wanting to "back" Clytia, — knowing how formidable my proud hostess could be, and, I feared, would be, — but the beautiful Caskian did not need my support. She was not timid. I never saw anything finer than her manner; the most consummate woman of the world could not have met the situation with more dignity and grace, and with not half so much simplicity. Her limpid dark eyes met Elodia's blue-rayed ones, and the result was mutual respect, with a slight giving on Elodia's part.

I felt that I had, for the first time in my life, seen a perfect woman; a woman of such fine proportions, of such nice balance, that her noble virtues and high intelligence did not make her forget even the smallest amenities. She kept in hand every faculty of her triple being, so that she was able to use each in its turn and to give to everything about her its due appreciation. She had, as Balzac says, the gift of admiration and of comprehension. That which her glance rested upon, that which her ear listened to, responded with all that was in them. I thought it a wonderful power that could so bring out the innate beauties and values of even inanimate things. Elodia's eyes rested upon her, from time to time, with a keen and questioning interest. I think that, among other things, she was surprised—as I was—at the elegance, the "style" even, of Clytia's dress.

Although there is very little fashion on that planet, as we know the word, there is a great deal of style. I had speedily mastered all its subtle gradations, and could "place" a woman with considerable certainty, by, let me say, her manner of wearing her clothes, if not the clothes themselves. I have never studied woman's apparel in detail, it always seems as mysterious to me as woman herself does; but I have a good eye for effects in that line, as most men have, and I knew that Clytia's costume was above criticism. She wore, just where they seemed to be needed,—as the keystone is needed in an arch,—a few fine gems. I could not conceive of her putting them on to arouse the envy of any other woman, or to enhance her personal charms in the eyes of a man. She dressed well, as another would sing well. Sight is the sense we value most, but how often is it offended! You can estimate the quality of a woman by the shade of green she chooses for her gown. And there is poetry in the fit of a gown, as there is in the color of it. Clytia knew these things, these higher principles of dress, as the nightingale knows its song, — through the effortless working of perfected faculties. But not she alone. My description of her will answer for the others; the Caskians are a people, you see, who neglect nothing. We upon the Earth are in the habit of saying, with regretful cadence, Life is short. It is because our life is all out of proportion. We are trying to cheat time; we stuff too much plunder into our bags, and discriminate against the best.

Clytia and Calypso and their friend Ariadne, a young girl, stayed with us throughout their visit; the others of their party were entertained elsewhere. On each of the two evenings they were with us, Elodia invited a considerable company of people, — not so many as to crowd the rooms, nor so few as to make them seem empty. Those gatherings were remarkable events, I imagine, in a good many lives.

They were in mine. At the close of each evening I retired to my room in a state of high mental intoxication; my unaccustomed brain had taken too large a draught of intellectual champagne. And when I awoke in the morning, it was with a sense of fatigue of mind, the same as one feels fatigue of body the day after extraordinary feats of physical exertion.

But not so the guests! who came down into the breakfast room as radiant as ever and in full possession of themselves. With them fatigue seemed impossible. We do not know — because we are so poorly trained — the wonderful elasticity of a human being, in all his parts. We often see it exemplified in single faculties, — the voice of a singer, the legs of a runner, the brain of a lawyer, the spirit of a religionist. But, as I have said before, we are all out of proportion, and any slight strain upon an unused faculty gives us the cramp. The fact is, the most of us are cripples in some sense. We lack a moral leg, a spiritual arm; there are parts of us that are neglected, withered, paralyzed.

One thing in the Caskians which especially pleased me, and which I am sure made a strong—and favorable—impression upon Elodia, too, was that their conduct and conversation never lacked the vital human interest without which all philosophy is cold, and all religion is asceticism.

It appeared that these people had taken the long journey not only to meet me, but that they might extend to me in person a cordial invitation to visit their country. Severnius warmly urged me to accept, assuring me, with unmistakable sincerity, that it would give him pleasure to put his purse at my disposal for the expenses of the journey,—I having brought up this point as a rather serious obstacle. As it would only add one more item to the great sum of my indebtedness to my friend, I took him at his word, and gave my promise to the Caskians to make the journey to Lunismar sometime in the near future. And with that they left us, and left behind them matter for conversation for many a day.

# CHAPTER 8.

## A TALK WITH ELODIA.

"It behoveth us also to consider the nature of him that offendeth."
— SENECA.

The longer I delayed my visit to Caskia, the more difficult it became for me to tear myself away from Thursia.
You may guess the lodestar that held me back. It was as if I were
attached to Elodia by an invisible chain which, alas! in no way
hindered her free movements, because she was unconscious of
its existence. Sometimes she treated me with a charmingly frank
*camaraderie,* and at other times her manner was simply, almost
coldly, courteous, — which I very well knew to be due to the fact
that she was more than usually absorbed in her business or official affairs; she was never cold for a purpose, any more than she
was fascinating for a purpose. She was singularly sincere, affect-
ing neither smiles nor frowns, neither affability nor severity, from
remote or calculating motives. In brief, she did not employ her
feminine graces, her sex-power, as speculating capital in social
commerce. The social conditions in Thursia do not demand that
women shall pose in a conciliatory attitude toward men — upon
whose favor their dearest privileges hang. Marriage not being

an economic necessity with them, they are released from certain sordid motives which often actuate women in our world in their frantic efforts to avert the appalling catastrophe of missing a husband; and they are at liberty to operate their matrimonial campaigns upon other grounds. I do not say higher grounds, because that I do not know. I only know that one base factor in the marriage problem, — the ignoble scheming to secure the means of living, as represented in a husband, — is eliminated, and the spirit of woman is that much more free.

We men have a feeling that we are liable at any time to be entrapped into matrimony by a mask of cunning and deceit, which heredity and long practice enable women to use with such amazing skill that few can escape it. We expect to be caught with chaff, like fractious colts coquetting with the halter and secretly not unwilling to be caught.

Another thing: woman's freedom to propose — which struck me as monstrous — takes away the reproach of her remaining single; the supposition being, as in the case of a bachelor, that it is a matter of choice with her. It saves her the dread of having it said that she has never had an opportunity to marry.

Courtship in Thursia may lack some of the tantalizing uncertainties which give it zest with us, but marriage also is robbed of many doubts and misgivings. Still I could not accustom myself with any feeling of comfort to the situation there, — the idea of masculine pre-eminence and womanly dependence being too thoroughly ingrained in my nature.

Elodia, of course, did many things and held many opinions of which I did not approve. But I believed in her innate nobility, and attributed her defects to a pernicious civilization and a government which did not exercise its paternal right to cherish, and restrain, and protect, the weaker sex, as they should be cherished, and restrained, and protected. And how charming and how reliable she was, in spite of her defects! She had an atomic weight upon which you could depend as upon any other known quantity. Her presence was a stimulus that quickened the faculties and intensified the emotions. At least I may speak for myself; she awoke new feelings and aroused new powers within me.

Her life had made her practical but not prosaic. She had imagination and poetic feeling; there were times when her beautiful countenance was touched with the grandeur of lofty thought, and again with the shifting lights of a playful humor, or the flashings of a keen but kindly wit. She had a laugh that mellowed the heart, as if she took you into her confidence. It is a mark of extreme favor when your superior, or a beautiful woman, admits you to the intimacy of a cordial laugh! Even her smiles, which I used to lie in wait for and often tried to provoke, were not the mere froth of a light and careless temperament; they had a significance like speech. Though she was so busy, and though she knew so well how to make the moments count, she could be idle when she chose, deliciously, luxuriously idle, — like one who will not fritter away his pence, but upon occasion spends his guineas handsomely. At the dinner hour she always gave us of her best. Her varied life supplies her with much material for conversation, — nothing worth noticing ever escaped her, in the life and conduct of people about her. She was fond of anecdote, and could garnish the simplest story with an exquisite grace.

Upon one of her idle days, — a day when Severnius happened not to be at home, — she took up her parasol in the hall after we had had luncheon, and gave me a glance which said, "Come with me if you like," and we went out and strolled through the grounds together. Her manner had not a touch of coquetry; I might have been simply another woman, she might have been simply another man. But I was so stupid as to essay little gallantries, such as had been, in fact, a part of my youthful education; she either did not observe them or ignored them, I could not tell which. Once I put out my hand to assist her over a ridiculously narrow streamlet, and she paid no heed to the gesture, but reefed her skirts, or draperies, with her own unoccupied hand and stepped lightly across. Again, when we were about to ascend an abrupt hill, I courteously offered her my arm.

"O, no, I thank you!" she said; "I have two, which balance me very well when I climb."

"You are a strange woman," I exclaimed with a blush.

"Am I?" she said, lifting her brows. "Well, I suppose — or rather you suppose — that I am the product of my ancestry and my training."

"You are, in some respects," I assented; and then I added, "I have often tried to fancy what effect our civilization would have had upon you."

"What effect do you think it would have had?" she asked, with quite an unusual — I might say earthly — curiosity.

"I dare not tell you," I replied, thrilling with the felicity of a talk so personal, — the first I had ever had with her.

"Why not?" she demanded, with a side glance at me from under her gold-fringed shade.

"It would be taking too great a liberty."

"But if I pardon that?" There was an archness in her smile which was altogether womanly. What a grand opportunity, I thought, for saying some of the things I had so often wanted to say to her! But I hesitated, turning hot and then cold.

"Really," I said, "I cannot. I should flatter you, and you would not like that."

For the first time, I saw her face crimson to the temples.

"That would be very bad taste," she replied; "flattery being the last resort—when it is found that there is nothing in one to compliment. Silence is better; you have commendable tact."

"Pardon my stupid blunder!" I cried; "you cannot think I meant that! Flattery is exaggerated, absurd, unmeaning praise, and no praise, the highest, the best, could do you justice, could—"

She broke in with a disdainful laugh:

"A woman can always compel a pretty speech from a man, you see,—even in Mars!"

"You did not compel it," I rejoined earnestly, "if I but dared,—if you would allow me to tell you what I think of you, how highly I regard—"

She made a gesture which cut short my eloquence, and we walked on in silence.

Whenever there has been a disturbance in the moral atmosphere, there is nothing like silence to restore the equilibrium. I, watching furtively, saw the slight cloud pass from her face, leaving the intelligent serenity it usually wore. But still she did not speak. However, there was nothing ominous in that, she was never troubled with an uneasy desire to keep conversation going.

On top of the hill there were benches, and we sat down. It was one of those still afternoons in summer when nature seems to be taking a siesta. Overhead it was like the heart of a rose. The soft, white, cottony clouds we often see suspended in our azure ether, floated—as soft, as white, as fleecy—in the pink skies of Mars.

Elodia closed her parasol and laid it across her lap and leaned her head back against the tree in whose shade we were. It was an acute pleasure, a rapture indeed, to sit so near to her and alone with her, out of hearing of all the world. But she was calmly unconscious, her gaze wandering dreamily through half-shut lids over the wide landscape, which included forests and fields and meadows, and many windings of the river, for we had a high point of observation.

I presently broke the silence with a bold, perhaps an inexcusable question,

"Elodia, do you intend ever to marry?"

It was a kind of challenge, and I held myself rigid, waiting for her answer, which did not come immediately. She turned her eyes toward me slowly without moving her head, and our glances met and gradually retreated, as two opposing forces might meet and retreat, neither conquering, neither vanquished. Hers went back into space, and she replied at last as if to space, — as if the question had come, not from me alone, but from all the voices that urge to matrimony.

"Why should I marry?"

"Because you are a woman," I answered promptly.

"Ah!" her lip curled with a faint smile, "your reason is very general, but why limit it at all, why not say because I am one of a pair which should be joined together?"

The question was not cynical, but serious; I scrutinized her face closely to make sure of that before answering.

"I know," I replied, "that here in Mars there is held to be no difference in the nature and requirements of the sexes, but it is a false hypothesis, there is a difference, — a vast difference! all my knowledge of humanity, my experience and observation, prove it."

"Prove it to you, no doubt," she returned, "but not to me, because my experience and observation have been the reverse of yours. Will you kindly tell me," she added, "why you think I should wish to marry any more than a man, — or what reasons can be urged upon a woman more than upon a man?"

An overpowering sense of helplessness fell upon me, — as when one has reached the limits of another's understanding and is unable to clear the ground for further argument.

"O, Elodia! I cannot talk to you," I replied. "It is true, as you say, that our conclusions are based upon diverse premises; we are so wide apart in our views on this subject that what I would say must seem to you the merest cant and sentiment."

"I think not; you are an honest man," she rejoined with an encouraging smile, "and I am greatly interested in your philosophy of marriage."

I acknowledged her compliment.

"Well," I began desperately, letting the words tumble out as they would, "it is woman's nature, as I understand it, to care a great deal about being loved, — loved wholly and entirely by one man who is worthy of her love, and to be united to him in the sacred bonds of marriage. To have a husband, children; to assume the sweet obligations of family ties, and to gather to herself the tenderest and purest affections humanity can know, is surely, indisputably, the best, the highest, noblest, province of woman."

"And not of man?"

"These things mean the same to men, of course," I replied, "though in lesser degree. It is man's office — with us — to buffet with the world, to wrest the means of livelihood, of comfort, luxury, from the grudging hand of fortune. It is the highest grace of woman that she accepts these things at his hands, she honors him in accepting, as he honors her in bestowing."

I was aware that I was indulging in platitudes, but the platitudes of Earth are novelties in Mars.

Her eyes took a long leap from mine to the vague horizon

line. "It is very strange," she said, "this distinction you make, I
cannot understand it at all. It seems to me that this love we are
talking about is simply one of the strong instincts implanted in
our common nature. It is an essential of our being. Marriage
is not, it is a social institution; and just why it is incumbent upon
one sex more than upon the other, or why it is more desirable
for one sex than the other, is inconceivable to me. If either a
man, or a woman, desires the ties you speak of, or if one has
the vanity to wish to found a respectable family, then, of course,
marriage is a necessity, — made so by our social and political laws.
It is a luxury we may have if we pay the price."

I was shocked at this cold-blooded reasoning, and cried, "O,
how can a woman say that! have you no tenderness, Elodia? no
heart-need of these ties and affections, — which I have always been
taught are so precious to woman?"

She shrugged her shoulders, and, leaning forward a little,
clasped her hands about her knees.

"Let us not make it personal," she said; "I admitted that these
things belong to our common nature, and I do not of course except myself. But I repeat that marriage is a convention, and —
I am not conventional."

"As to that," I retorted, "all the things that pertain to civilization, all the steps which have ever been taken in the direction
of progress, are conventions: our clothing, our houses, our religions, arts, our good manners. And we are bound to accept every
'convention' that makes for the betterment of society, as though
it were a revelation from God."

I confess that this thought was the fruit of my brief intercourse with the Caskians, who hold that there is a divine power
continually operating upon human consciousness, — not disclos-

ing miracles, but enlarging and perfecting human perceptions. I was thinking of this when Elodia suddenly put the question to me:

"Are you married?"

"No, I am not," I replied. The inquiry was not agreeable to me; it implied that she had been hitherto altogether too indifferent as to my "eligibility," — never having concerned herself to ascertain the fact before.

"Well, you are perhaps older than I am," she said, "and you have doubtless had amours?"

I was as much astounded by the frankness of this inquiry as you can be, and blushed like a girl. She withdrew her eyes from my face with a faint smile and covered the question by another:

"You intend to marry, I suppose?"

"I do, certainly," I replied, the resolution crystallizing on the instant.

She drew a long sigh. "Well, I do not, I am so comfortable as I am." She patted the ground with her slipper toe. "I do not wish to impose new conditions upon myself. I simply accept my life as it comes to me. Why should I voluntarily burden myself with a family, and all the possible cares and sorrows which attend the marriage state! If I cast a prophetic eye into the future, what am I likely to see? — Let us say, a lovely daughter dying of some frightful malady; an idolized son squandering my wealth and going to ruin; a husband in whom I no longer delight, but to whom I am bound by a hundred intricate ties impossible to sever. I think I am not prepared to take the future on trust to so great an extent! Why should the free wish for fetters? Affection and sympathy are good things, indispensable things in fact, — but I find them in my friends. And for this other matter: this need of love, passion, sentiment, — which is peculiarly ephemeral in its impulses, notwithstanding that it has such an insistent vitality in the human heart, — may be satisfied without entailing such tremendous responsibilities."

I looked at her aghast; did she know what she was saying; did she mean what her words implied?

"You wrong yourself, Elodia," said I; "those are the sentiments, the arguments, of a selfish person, of a mean and cowardly spirit. And you have none of those attributes; you are strong, courageous, generous —"

"You mistake me," she interrupted, "I am entirely selfish; I do not wish to disturb my present agreeable pose. Tell me, what is it that usually prompts people to marry?"

"Why, love, of course," I answered.

"Well, you are liable to fall in love with my maid —"

"Not after having seen her mistress!" I ejaculated.

"If she happens to possess a face or figure that draws your masculine eye," she went on, the rising color in her cheek responding to my audacious compliment; "though there may be nothing in common between you, socially, intellectually, or spiritually. What would be the result of such a marriage, based upon simple sex-love?"

I had known many such marriages, and was familiar with the results, but I did not answer. We tacitly dropped the subject, and our two minds wandered away as they would, on separate currents.

She was the first to break this second silence.

"I can conceive of a marriage," she said, "which would not become burdensome, any more than our best friendships become burdensome. Beside the attraction on the physical plane — which I believe is very necessary — there should exist all the higher affinities. I should want my husband to be my most delightful companion, able to keep my liking and to command my respect and confidence as I should hope to his. But I fear that is ideal."

"The ideal is only the highest real," I answered, "the ideal is always possible."

"Remotely!" she said with a laugh. "The chances are many against it."

"But even if one were to fall short a little in respect to husband or wife, I have often observed that there are compensations springing out of the relation, in other ways," I returned.

"You mean children? O, yes, that is true, when all goes well. I will tell you," she added, her voice dropping to the tone one instantly recognizes as confidential, "that I am educating several children in some of our best schools, and that I mean to provide for them with sufficient liberality when they come of age. So, you see, I have thrown hostages to fortune and shall probably reap a harvest of gratitude, — in place of filial affection."

She laughed with a touch of mockery.

I suppose every one is familiar with the experience of having things — facts, bits of knowledge, — "come" to him, as we say. Something came to me, and froze the marrow in my bones.

"Elodia," I ventured, "you asked me a very plain question a moment ago, will you forgive me if I ask you the same, — have you had amours?"

The expression of her face changed slightly, which might have been due to the expression of mine.

"We have perhaps grown too frank with each other," she said, "but you are a being from another world, and that must excuse us, — shall it?"

I bowed, unable to speak.

"One of the children I spoke of, a little girl of six, is my own natural child."

She made this extraordinary confession with her glance fixed steadily upon mine.

I am a man of considerable nerve, but for a moment the world was dark to me and I had the sensation of one falling from a great height. And then suddenly relief came to me in the thought, She is not to be judged by the standards that measure morality in my country! When I could command my voice again I asked:

"Does this little one know that she is your child, — does any one else know?"

"Certainly not," she answered in a tone of surprise, and then with an ironical smile, "I have treated you to an exceptional confidence. It is a matter of etiquette with us to keep these things hidden."

As I made no response she added:

"Is it a new thing to you for a parent not to acknowledge illegitimate children?"

"Even the lowest class of mothers we have on Earth do not often abandon their offspring," I replied.

"Neither do they here," she said. "The lowest class have nothing to gain and nothing to lose, and consequently there is no necessity that they should sacrifice their natural affections. In this respect, the lower classes are better off than we aristocrats."

"You beg the question," I returned; "you know what I mean! I should not have thought that you, Elodia, could ever be moved by such unworthy considerations — that you would ever fear the world's opinions! you who profess manly qualities, the noblest of which is courage!"

"Am I to understand by that," she said, "that men on your

planet acknowledge their illegitimate progeny, and allow them
the privileges of honored sons and daughters?"

Pushed to this extremity, I could recall but a single instance, — but one man whose courage and generosity, in a case
of the kind under discussion, had risen to the level of his crime.
I related to her the story of his splendid and prolonged life, with
its one blot of early sin, and its grace of practical repentance.
And upon the other hand, I told her of the one distinguished
modern woman, who has had the hardihood to face the world
with her offenses in her hands, as one might say.

"Are you not rather unjust to the woman?" she asked. "You
speak of the man's acknowledgment of his sin as something fine,
and you seem to regard hers as simply impudent."

"Because of the vast difference between the moral attitude
of the two," I rejoined. "He confessed his error and took his punishment with humility; she slaps society in the face, and tries
to make her genius glorify her misdeeds."

"Possibly society is to blame for that, by setting her at bay.
If I have got the right idea about your society, it is as unrelenting
to the one sex as it is indulgent to the other. Doubtless it was
ready with open arms to receive back the offending, repentant
man, but would it not have set its foot upon the woman's neck
if she had given it the chance, if she had knelt in humility as
he did? A tree bears fruit after its kind; so does a code of morals.
Gentleness and forgiveness breed repentance and reformation,
and harshness begets defiance." She added with a laugh, "What
a spectacle your civilization would present if all the women who
have sinned had the genius and the spirit of a Bernhardt!"

"Or all the men had the magnanimity of a Franklin," I
retorted.

"True!" she said, and after a moment she continued, "I am

not so great as the one, nor have I the 'effrontery' of the other. But it is not so much that I lack courage; it is rather, perhaps, a delicate consideration for, and concession to, the good order of society."

I regarded her with amazement, and she smiled.

"Really, it is true," she said. "I believe in social order and I pay respect to it —"

"By concealing your own transgressions," I interpolated.

"Well, why not? Suppose I and my cult — a very large class of eminently respectable sinners! — should openly trample upon this time-honored convention; the result would eventually be, no doubt, a moral anarchy. We have a very clear sense of our responsibility to the masses. We make the laws for their government, and we allow ourselves to seem to be governed by them also, — so that they may believe in them. We build churches and pay pew rent, though we do not much believe in the religious dogmas. And we leave off wine when we entertain temperance people."

"But why do you do these things?" I asked; "to what end?"

"Simply for the preservation of good order and decency. You must know that the pleasant vices of an elegant person are brutalities in the uncultured. The masses have no tact or delicacy, they do not comprehend shades and refinements of morals and manners. They can understand exoteric but not esoteric philosophy. We have really two codes of laws."

"I think it would be far better for the masses — whom you so highly respect! —" I said, "if you were to throw off your masks and stand out before them just as you are. Let moral anarchy come if it must, and the evil be consumed in its own flame; out of its ashes the phœnix always rises again, a nobler bird."

"How picturesque!" she exclaimed; "do you know, I think

your language must be rich in imagery. I should like to learn it."

I did not like the flippancy of this speech, and made no reply.

After a brief pause she added, "There is truth in what you say, a ball must strike hard before it can rebound. Society must be fearfully outraged before it turns upon the offender, if he be a person of consequence. But you cannot expect the offender to do his worst, to dash himself to pieces, in order that a better state of morals may be built upon his ruin. We have not yet risen to such sublimity of devotion and self-sacrifice. I think the fault and the remedy both, lie more with the good people, — the people who make a principle of moral conduct. They allow us to cajole them into silence, they wink at our misdeeds. They know what we are up to, but they conceal the knowledge, — heaven knows why! — as carefully as we do our vices. Contenting themselves with breaking out in general denunciations which nobody accepts as personal rebuke."

This was such a familiar picture that for a moment I fancied myself upon the Earth again. And I thought, what a difficult position the good have to maintain everywhere, for having accepted the championship of a cause whose standards are the highest and best! We expect them to be wise, tender, strong, just, stern, merciful, charitable, unyielding, forgiving, sinless, fearless.

"Elodia," I said presently, "you can hardly understand what a shock this — this conversation has been to me. I started out with saying that I had often tried to fancy what our civilization might have done for you. I see more clearly now. You are the victim of the harshest and cruelest assumption that has ever been upheld concerning woman, — that her nature is no finer, holier than man's. I have reverenced womanhood all my life as the highest, and purest thing under heaven, and I will, I must, hold fast to that faith, to that rock on which the best traditions of our Earth are founded."

"Do your women realize what they have got to live up to?" she asked ironically.

"There are things in men which offset their virtues," I returned, in justice to my own sex. "Where men are strong, women are gentle, where women are faithful, men are brave, and so on."

"How charming to have the one nature dovetail into the other so neatly!" she exclaimed. "I seem to see a vision, shall I tell it to you,—a vision of your Earth? In the Beginning, you know that is the way in which all our traditions start out, there was a great heap of Qualities stacked in a pyramid upon the Earth. And the human creatures were requested to step up and help themselves to such as suited their tastes. There was a great scramble, and your sex, having some advantages in the way of muscle and limb,—and not having yet acquired the arts of courtesy and gallantry for which you are now so distinguished,—pressed forward and took first choice. Naturally you selected the things which were agreeable to possess in themselves, and the exercise of which would most redound to your glory; such virtues as chastity, temperance, patience, modesty, piety, and some minor graces, were thrust aside and eventually forced upon the weaker sex,—since it was necessary that all the Qualities should be used in order to make a complete Human Nature. Is not that a pretty fable?"

She arose and shook out her draperies and spread her parasol. There were crimson spots in her cheeks, I felt that I had angered her,—and on the other hand, she had outraged my finest feelings. But we were both capable of self-government.

"It must be near dinner time," she said, quietly.

I walked along by her side in silence.

As we again crossed the brooklet, she stooped and picked a long raceme of small white, delicately odorous flowers, and together we analyzed them, and I recognized them as belonging to our family of *convallaria majalis*. This led to a discussion of comparative botany on the two planets, — a safe, neutral topic. In outward appearance our mutual attitude was unchanged. Inwardly, there had been to me something like the moral upheaval of the universe. For the first time I had melancholy symptoms of nostalgia, and passionately regretted that I had ever exchanged the Earth for Mars.

Severnius had returned. After dinner he invited me out onto the veranda to smoke a cigar, — he was very particular not to fill the house with tobacco smoke. Elodia, he said, did not like the odor. I wondered whether he took such pains out of consideration for her, or whether he simply dreaded her power to retaliate with her obnoxious vapor. The latter supposition, however, I immediately repudiated as being unjust to him; he was the gentlest and sweetest of men.

My mind was so full of the subject Elodia and I had discussed that I could not forbear repeating my old question to him:

"Tell me, my friend," I entreated, "do you in your inmost soul believe that men and women have one common nature, — that women are no better at all than men, and that men may, if they will, be as pure as — well, as women ought to be?"

Severnius smiled. "If you cannot find an answer to your first question here in Paleveria, I think you may in any of the savage countries, where I am quite positive the women exhibit no finer qualities than their lords. And for a very conclusive reply to your second question, — go to Caskia!"

"Does the same idea of equality, or likeness rather, exist in Caskia that prevails here?" I asked.

"O, yes," said he, "but their plane of life is so much higher. I cannot but believe in the equality," he added, "bad as things are with us. We hope that we are progressing onward and upward; all our teaching and preaching tend toward that, as you may find in our churches and schools, and in our literature. I am so much of an optimist as to believe that we are getting better and better all the time. One evidence is that there is less of shamelessness than there used to be with respect to some of the grossest offences against decency. People do not now glory in their vices, they hide them."

"Then you approve of concealment!" I exclaimed.

"It is better than open effrontery, it shows that the moral power in society is the stronger; that it is making the way of the transgressor hard, driving him into dark corners."

I contrasted this in my mind with Elodia's theory on the same subject. The two differed, but there was a certain harmony after all.

Severnius added, apropos of what had gone before, "It does not seem fair to me that one half of humanity should hang upon the skirts of the other half; it is better that we should go hand in hand, even though our progress is slow."

"But that cannot be," I returned; "there are always some that must bear the burden while others drag behind."

"O, certainly; that is quite natural and right," he assented. "The strong should help the weak. What I mean is that we should not throw the burden upon any particular class, or allow to any particular class special indulgences. That — pardon me! — is the fault I find with your civilization; you make your women the chancellors of virtue, and claim for your sex the privilege of being virtuous or not, as you choose." He smiled as he added, "Do you know, your loyalty and tender devotion to individual women, and your antagonistic attitude toward women in general — on the moral plane. — presents the most singular contrast to my mind!"

"No doubt," I said; "it is a standing joke with us. We are better in the sample than in the whole piece. As individuals, we are woman's devoted slaves, and lovers, and worshipers; as a political body, we are her masters, from whom she wins grudging concessions; as a social factor, we refuse her dictation."

I was not in a mood to discuss the matter further. I was sick at heart and angry, — not so much with Elodia as with the conditions that had made her what she was, a woman perfect in every other respect, but devoid of the one supreme thing, — the sense of virtue. She was now to me simply a splendid ruin, a temple without holiness. I went up to my room and spent the night plunged in the deepest sadness I had ever known. When one is suffering an insupportable agony, he catches at the flimsiest delusions for momentary relief. He says to himself, "My friend is not dead!" "My beloved is not false!" So I tried to cheat myself. I argued, "Why, this is only a matter of education with me, surely; how many women, with finer instincts than mine, have loved and married men of exactly the same stamp as Elodia!" But I put away the thought with a shudder, feeling that it would be a far more dreadful thing to relax my principles and to renounce my faith in woman's purity than to sacrifice my love. The tempter came in another form. Suppose she should repent? But my soul revolted. No, no; Jesus might pardon a Magdalene, but I could not. Elodia was dead; Elodia had never been! That night I buried her; I said I would never look upon her face again. But the morning brought resurrection. How hard a thing it is to destroy love!

# CHAPTER 9.

## JOURNEYING UPWARD.

"The old order changeth, giving place to the new,
And God fulfils himself in many ways." — TENNYSON.

**M**y conversation with Elodia had the effect of crystallizing my nebulous plans about visiting the Caskians into
a sudden resolve. I could not remain longer in her presence without pain to myself; and, to tell the truth, I dreaded lest her as-
tounding lack of the moral sense — which should be the foundation
stone of woman's character — would eventually dull my own. Men
are notoriously weak where women are concerned — the women
they worship.

As soon as I had communicated with the Caskians and learned
that they were still anticipating my coming, with — they were so
kind as to say it — the greatest pleasure, I prepared to set forth.

In the meantime, an event occurred which further illustrated
the social conditions in Paleveria. Claris, the wife of Massilla,
died very suddenly, and I was astonished at the tremendous sensation the circumstance occasioned throughout the city. It seemed
to me that the only respect it was possible to pay to the memory
of such a woman must be that which is expressed in absolute

silence,—even charity could not be expected to do more than keep silent. But I was mistaken, Claris had been a woman of distinction, in many ways; she was beautiful, rich, and talented, and she had wielded an influence in public and social affairs. Immediately, the various periodicals in Thursia, and in neighboring cities, flaunted lengthy eulogistic obituaries headed with more or less well executed portraits of the deceased. It seemed as if the authors of these effusions must have run through dictionaries of complimentary terms, which they culled lavishly and inserted among the acts and facts of her life with a kind of journalistic sleight-of-hand. And private comment took its cue from these authorities. It was said that she was a woman of noble traits, and pretty anecdotes were told of her, illustrating her generous impulses, her wit, her positiveness. She had had great personal magnetism, many had loved her, many had also feared her, for her tongue could cut like a sword. It was stated that her children had worshiped her, and that her death had prostrated her husband with grief. Of the chief blackness of her character none spoke.

Severnius invited me to attend the funeral obsequies which took place in the Auroras' Temple, where the embalmed body lay in state; with incense burning and innumerable candles casting their pallid light upon the bier. I observed as we drove through the streets that the closed doors of all the business houses exhibited the emblems of respect and sorrow.

The Auroras were assembled in great numbers, having come from distant parts of the country to do honor to the dead. They were in full regalia, with mourning badges, and carried inverted torches. The religious ceremonies and mystic rites of the Order were elaborate and impressive. The dirge which followed, and during which the members of the Order formed in procession and began a slow march, was so unutterably and profoundly sad that I could not keep back the tears. A little sobbing voice directly in front of me wailed out "Mamma! Mamma!" A woman stooped down and whispered, "Do you want to go up and kiss Mamma 'good-by' before they take her away?" But the child shrank back, afraid of the pomp and ghostly magnificence surrounding the dead form.

Elodia was of course the chief figure in the procession, and she bore herself with a grave and solemn dignity in keeping with the ceremonies. The sight of her beautiful face, with its subdued but lofty expression, was more than I could bear. I leaned forward and dropped my face in my hands, and let the sorrow-laden requiem rack my soul with its sweet torture as it would.

That was my last day in Thursia.

I had at first thought of taking my aeroplane along with me, reflecting that I might better begin my homeward flight from some mountain top in Caskia; but Severnius would not hear of that.

"No indeed!" said he, "you must return to us again. I wish to get ready a budget for you to carry back to your astronomers, which I think will be of value to them, as I shall make a complete map of the heavens as they appear to us. Then we shall be eager to hear about your visit. And besides, we want to see you again on the ground of friendship, the strongest reason of all!"

"You are too kind!" I responded with much feeling. I knew that he was as sincere as he was polite. This was at the last moment, and Elodia was present to bid me "good-by." She seconded her brother's invitation, — "O, yes, of course you must come back!" and turned the whole power of her beautiful face upon me, and for the first time gave me her hand. I had coveted it a hundred times as it lay lissome and white in her lap. I clasped it, palm to palm. It was as smooth as satin, and not moist, — I dislike a moist hand. I felt that up to that moment I had always under-valued the sense of touch, — it was the finest of all the senses! No music, no work of art, no wondrous scene, had ever so thrilled me and set my nerves a-quiver, as did the delicate, firm pressure of those magic fingers. The remembrance of it made my blood tingle as I went on my long journey from Thursia to Lunismar.

It was a long journey in miles, though not in time, we trav-eled like the wind.

Both Clytia and Calypso were at the station to meet me, with their two children, Freya and Eurydice. I learned that nearly all Caskians are named after the planetoids or other heavenly bodies, —a very appropriate thing, since they live so near the stars!

My heart went out to the children the moment my eyes fell upon their faces.

They were as beautiful as Raphael's cherubs, you could not look upon them without thrills of delight. They were two perfect buds of the highest development humanity has ever attained to, — so far as we know. I felt that it was a wonderful thing to know that in these lovely forms there lurked no germs of evil, over their sweet heads there hung no Adam's curse! They were seated in a pretty pony carriage, with a white canopy top lined with blue silk. Freya held the lines. It appeared that Eurydice had driven down and he was to drive back. The father and mother were on foot. They explained that it was difficult to drive anything but the little carriage up the steep path to their home on the hillside, half a mile distant.

"Who would wish for any other means of locomotion than nature has given him, in a country where the buoyant air makes walking a luxury!" I cried, stretching my legs and filling my lungs, with an unwonted sense of freedom and power.

I had become accustomed to the atmosphere of Paleveria,

but here I had the same sensations I had experienced when I first landed there.

"If you would rather, you may take my place, sir?" said the not much more than knee-high Freya, ready to relinquish the lines. I felt disposed to laugh, but not so the wise parents.

"The little ponies could not draw our friend up the hill, he is too heavy," explained Clytia.

"Thank you, my little man, all the same!" I added.

It was midsummer in Paleveria, but here I observed everything had the newness and delightful freshness of spring. A busy, bustling, joyous, tuneful spring. The grass was green and succulent; the sap was in the trees and their bark was sleek and glossy, their leaves just unrolled. Of the wild fruit trees, every branch and twig was loaded with eager buds crowding upon each other as the heads of children crowd at a cottage window when one goes by. Every thicket was full of bird life and music. I heard the roar of a waterfall in the distance, and Calypso told me that a mighty river, the Eudosa, gathered from a hundred mountain streams, was compressed into a deep gorge or canyon and fell in a succession of cataracts just below the city, and finally spread out into a lovely lake, which was a wonder in its way, being many fathoms deep and as transparent as the atmosphere.

We paused to listen, — the children also.

"How loud it is to-day, Mamma," exclaimed Freya. His mother assented and turned to me with a smile. "The falls of Eudosa constitute a large part of our life up here," she said; "we note all its moods, which are many. Sometimes it is drowsy, and purrs and murmurs; again it is merry, and sings; or it is sublime, and rises to a thunderous roar. Always it is sound. Do you know, my ears ached with the silence when I was down in Paleveria!"

I have said Clytia's eyes were black; it was not an opaque

blackness, you could look through them down into her soul. I likened them in my mind to the waters of the Eudosa which Calypso had just described.

Every moment something new attracted our attention and the brief journey was full of incident; the children were especially alive to the small happenings about us, and I never before took such an interest in what I should have called insignificant things. Sometimes the conversation between my two friends and myself rose above the understanding of the little ones, but they were never ignored, — nor were they obtrusive; they seemed to know just where to fit their little questions and remarks into the talk. It was quite wonderful. I understood, of course, that the children had been brought down to meet me in order that I might make their acquaintance immediately and establish my relations with them, since I was to be for some time a member of the household. They had their small interests apart from their elders — carefully guarded by their elders — as children should have; but whenever they were permitted to be with us, they were of us. They were never allowed to feel that loneliness in a crowd which is the most desolate loneliness in the world. Clytia especially had the art of enveloping them in her sympathy, though her intellectual faculties were employed elsewhere. And how they loved her! I have seen nothing like it upon the Earth.

Perhaps I adapt myself with unusual readiness to new environments, and assimilate more easily with new persons than most people do. I had, as you know, left Paleveria with deep reluctance, under compulsion of my will — moved by my better judgment; and throughout my journey I had deliberately steeped myself in sweet and bitter memories of my life there, to the exclusion of much that might have been interesting and instructive to me on the way, — a foolish and childish thing to have done. And now, suddenly, Paleveria dropped from me like a garment. Some moral power in these new friends, and perhaps in this city of Lunismar,—a power I could feel but could not define,—raised me to a different, unmistakably a higher, plane. I felt the change as one feels the change from underground to the upper air.

We first walked a little way through the city, which quite filled the valley and crept up onto the hillsides, here and there.

Each building stood alone, with a little space of ground around it, upon which grass and flowers and shrubbery grew, and often trees. Each such space bore evidence that it was as tenderly and scrupulously tended as a Japanese garden.

It was the cleanest city I ever saw; there was not an unsightly place, not a single darksome alley or lurking place for vice, no huddling together of miserable tenements. I remarked upon this and Calypso explained:

"Our towns used to be compact, but since electricity has annihilated distance we have spread ourselves out. We have plenty of ground for our population, enough to give a generous slice all round. Lunismar really extends through three valleys."

Crystal streams trickled down from the mountains and were utilized for practical and æsthetic purposes. Small parks, exquisitely pretty, were very numerous, and in them the sparkling water was made to play curious pranks. Each of these spots was an ideal resting place, and I saw many elderly people enjoying them,— people whom I took to be from sixty to seventy years of age, but who, I was astonished to learn, were all upwards of a hundred. Perfect health and longevity are among the rewards of right living practiced from generation to generation. The forms of these old people were erect and their faces were beautiful in intelligence and sweetness of expression.

I remarked, apropos of the general beauty and elegance of the buildings we passed:

"This must be the fine quarter of Lunismar."

"No, not especially," returned Calypso, "it is about the same all over."

"Is it possible! then you must all be rich?" said I.

"We have no very poor," he replied, "though of course some have larger possessions than others. We have tried, several times in the history of our race, to equalize the wealth of the country, but the experiment has always failed, human nature varies so much."

"What, even here?" I asked.

"What do you mean?" said he.

"Why, I understand that you Caskians have attained to a most perfect state of development and culture, and —" I hesitated and he smiled.

"And you think the process eliminates individual traits?" he inquired.

Clytia laughingly added:

"I hope, sir, you did not expect to find us all exactly alike, that would be too tame!"

"You compliment me most highly," said Calypso, seriously, "but we must not permit you to suppose that we regard our 'development' as anywhere near perfect, In fact, the farther we advance, the greater, and the grander, appears the excellence to which we have not yet attained. Though it would be false modesty—and a disrespect to our ancestors—not to admit that we are conscious of having made some progress, as a race. We know what our beginnings were, and what we now are."

After a moment he went on:

"I suppose the principle of differentiation, as we observe it in plant and animal life, is the same in all life, not only physical, but intellectual, moral, spiritual. Cultivation, though it softens salient traits and peculiarities, may develop infinite variety in every kind and species."

I understood this better later on, after I had met a greater number of people, and after my perceptions had become more delicate and acute, — or when a kind of initiatory experience had taught me how to see and to value excellence.

A few years ago a border of nasturtiums exhibited no more than a single color tone, the pumpkin yellow; and a bed of pansies resembled a patch of purple heather. Observe now the chromatic variety and beauty produced by intelligent horticulture! A group of commonplace people — moderately disciplined by culture — might be compared to the pansies and nasturtiums of our early recollection, and a group of these highly refined Caskians to the delicious flowers abloom in modern gardens.

We crave variety in people, as we crave condiments in food. For me, this craving was never so satisfied — and at the same time so thoroughly stimulated — as in Caskian society, which had a spiciness of flavor impossible to describe.

Formality was disarmed by perfect breeding, there was nothing that you could call "manner." The delicate faculty of intuition produced harmony. I never knew a single instance in which the social atmosphere was disagreeably jarred, — a common enough occurrence where we depend upon the machinery of social order rather than upon the vital principle of good conduct.

I inquired of Calypso, as we walked along, the sources of the people's wealth. He replied that the mountains were full of it. There were minerals and precious stones, and metals in great abundance; and all the ores were manufactured in the vicinity of the mines before being shipped to the lower countries and exchanged for vegetable products.

This prompted me to ask the familiar question:

"And how do you manage the labor problem?" He did not understand me until after I had explained about our difficulties in that line. And then he informed me that most of the people who worked in mines and factories had vested interests in them.

"Physical labor, however," he added, "is reduced to the minimum; machinery has taken the place of muscle."

"And thrown an army of workers out of employment and the means of living, I suppose?" I rejoined, taking it for granted that the small share-holders had been squeezed out, as well as the small operators.

"O, no, indeed," he returned, in surprise. "It has simply given them more leisure. Everybody now enjoys the luxury of spare time, and may devote his energies to the service of other than merely physical needs." He smiled as he went on, "This labor problem the Creator gave us was a knotty one, wasn't it? But what a tremendous satisfaction there is in the thought — and in the fact — that we have solved it."

I was in the dark now, and waited for him to go on.

"To labor incessantly, to strain the muscles, fret the mind, and weary the soul, and to shorten the life, all for the sake of supplying the wants of the body, and nothing more, is, I think, an inconceivable hardship. And to have invoked the forces of the insensate elements and laid our burdens upon them, is a glorious triumph."

"Yes, if all men are profited by it," I returned doubtfully.

"They are, of course," said he, "at least with us. I was shocked to find it quite different in Paleveria. There, it seemed to me, machinery—which has been such a boon to the laborers here—has been utilized simply and solely to increase the wealth of the rich. I saw a good many people who looked as though they were on the brink of starvation."

"I don't see how you manage it otherwise," I confessed.

"It belongs to the history of past generations," he replied. "Perhaps the hardest struggle our progenitors had was to conquer the lusts of the flesh,—of which the greed of wealth is doubtless the greatest. They began to realize, generations ago, that Mars was rich enough to maintain all his children in comfort and even luxury,—that none need hunger, or thirst, or go naked or houseless, and that more than this was vanity and vain-glory. And just as they, with intense assiduity, sought out and cultivated nature's resources—for the reduction of labor and the increase of wealth—so they sought out and cultivated within themselves corresponding resources, those fit to meet the new era of material prosperity; namely, generosity and brotherly love."

"Then you really and truly practice what you preach!" said I, with scant politeness, and I hastened to add, "Severnius told me that you recognize the trinity in human nature. Well, we do, too, upon the Earth, but the Three have hardly an equal chance! We preach the doctrine considerably more than we practice it."

"I understand that you are a highly intellectual people," remarked Calypso, courteously.

"Yes, I suppose we are," said I; "our achievements in that line are nothing to be ashamed of. And," I added, remembering some felicitous sensations of my own, "there is no greater delight than the travail of intellect which brings forth great ideas."

"Pardon me!" he returned, "the travail of soul which brings

forth a great love — a love willing to share equally with others the fruits of intellectual triumph — is, to my mind, infinitely greater."

We had reached the terrace, or little plateau, on which my friends' house stood; it was like a strip of green velvet for color and smoothness.

The house was built of rough gray stone which showed silver glintings in the sun. Here and there, delicate vines clung to the walls. There was a carriage porch — into which the children drove — and windows jutting out into the light, and many verandas and little balconies, that seemed to give the place a friendly and hospitable air. Above there was a spacious observatory, in which was mounted a very fine telescope that must have cost a fortune, — though my friends were not enormously rich, as I had learned from Severnius. But these people do not regard the expenditure of even very large sums of money for the means of the best instruction and the best pleasures as extravagance, if no one suffers in consequence. I cannot go into their economic system very extensively here, but I may say that it provides primarily that all shall share bountifully in the general good; and after that, individuals may gratify their respective tastes — or rather, satisfy their higher needs; for their tastes are never fanciful, but always real — as they can afford.

I do not mean that this is a written law, a formal edict, to be evaded by such cunning devices as we know in our land, or at best loosely construed; nor is it a mere sentiment preached from pulpits and glorified in literature, — a beautiful but impracticable conception! It is purely a moral law, and being such it is a vital principle in each individual consciousness.

The telescope was Calypso's dearest possession, but I never doubted his willingness to give it up, if there should come a time when the keeping of it would be the slightest infringement of this law. I may add that in all the time I spent in Caskia, I never saw a man, woman, or child, but whose delight in any possession would have been marred by the knowledge that his, or her, gratification meant another's bitter deprivation. The question between Thou and I was always settled in favor of Thou. And no barriers of race, nationality, birth, or position, affected this universal principle.

I made a discovery in relation to the Caskians which would have surprised and disappointed me under most circumstances; they had no imagination, and they were not given to emotional excitation. Their minds touched nothing but what was real. But mark this: Their real was our highest ideal. The moral world was to them a real world; the spiritual world was to them a real world. They had no need of imagery. And they were never carried away by floods of feeling, for they were always up to their highest level, — I mean in the matter of kindness and sympathy and love. Moreover, their intellectual perceptions were so clear, and the mysteries of nature were unrolled before their understanding in such orderly sequence, that although their increase of knowledge was a continuous source of delight, it never came in shocks of surprise or excited childish wonderment. I cannot hope to give you more than a faint conception of the dignity and majesty of a people whose triple nature was so highly and so harmoniously developed. One principle governed the three: Truth. They were true to every law under which they had been created and by which they were sustained. They were taught from infancy — but of this further on. I wish to reintroduce Ariadne to you and let her explain some of the wonders of their teaching, she being herself a teacher.

The observatory was a much used apartment, by both the

family and by guests. It was a library also, and it contained musical instruments. A balcony encircled it on the outside, and here we often sat of evenings, especially if the sky was clear and the stars and moon were shining. The heavens as seen at night were as familiar to Clytia and Calypso, and even to the children, as a friend's face.

It was pleasant to sit out upon the balcony even on moonless nights and when the stars were hidden, and look down upon the city all brilliantly alight, and listen to the unceasing music of the Falls of Eudosa. I, too, soon learned his many "moods."

Back of the house there rose a long succession of hills, ending finally in snowcapped mountains, the highest of which was called the Spear, so sharply did it thrust its head up through the clouds into the heavens.

The lower hills had been converted into vineyards. A couple of men were fixing the trellises, the Calypso excused himself to his wife and me and went over to them. A neatly dressed maid came out of the house and greeted the children, who had much important news to relate concerning their drive; and a last year's bird-nest to show her, which they took pains to explain was quite useless to the birds, who were all making nice new nests. The sight of the maid, — evidently an intelligent and well-bred girl, — whose face beamed affectionately upon the little ones, prompted a question from me:

"How do you manage about your servants, I mean house servants," I asked; "do you have people here who are willing to do menial work?"

Clytia looked up at me with an odd expression. Her answer, coming from any one less sincere, would have sounded like cant.

"We do not regard any work as mean."

"But some kinds of work are distasteful, to say the least," I insisted.

"Not if you love those for whom you labor," she returned. "A mother does not consider any sort of service to her child degrading."

"O, I know that," said I; "that is simply natural affection."

"But natural affection, you know, is only the germ of love. It is narrow,—only a little broader than selfishness."

"Well, tell me how it applies in this question of service?" I asked. "I am not able to comprehend it in the abstract."

"We do not require people to do anything for us which we would not do for ourselves, or for them," she said. "And then, we all work. We believe in work; it means strength to the body and relief to the mind. No one permits himself to be served by another for the unworthy reason, openly or tacitly confessed, that he is either too proud, or too indolent, to serve himself."

"Then why have servants at all?" I asked.

"My husband explained to you," she returned, "that our people are not all equally rich; and they are not all adapted to what you would call, perhaps, the higher grades of service. You see the little maid yonder with the children; she has the gifts of a teacher,—our teachers are very carefully chosen, and as carefully instructed. She has been placed with me for our mutual benefit,—I could not intrust my little ones to the care of a mere paid nurse who thought only of her wages. Nor could she work simply for wages. The money consideration is the smallest item in the arrangement. My husband superintends some steel works in which he has some shares. The man he is talking with now— who is attending to the grape vines—has also a large interest in the steel works, but he has no taste or faculty for engaging in that kind of business. He might spend his whole life in idleness if he chose, or in mental pursuits, for he is a very scholarly man, but he loves the kind of work he is doing now, and our vineyard is his especial pride. Moreover," a beautiful smile touched her face as she looked up at the two men on the hillside, "Fides loves my Calypso, they are soul friends!"

When I became more familiar with the household, I found that the same relations existed all round; mutual pleasure, mutual sympathy, mutual helpfulness. First there seemed to be on the part of each employee a distinct preference and liking for the kind of work he or she had undertaken to do; second, a fitness and careful preparation for the work; and last, the love of doing for those who gave appreciation, love, and another sort of service or assistance in return. I heard one of them say one day:

"I ask nothing better than to be permitted to cook the meals for these dear people!"

This was a woman who wrote monthly articles on chemistry and botany for one of the leading scientific journals. She was a middle-aged woman and unmarried, who did not wish to live alone, who abhorred "boarding," and who had found just such a comfortable nest in Clytia's home as suited all her needs and desires. Of course she did not slave in the kitchen all day long, and her position did not debar her from the best and most intelligent society, nor cut her off from the pleasure and privileges that sweeten life. She brought her scientific knowledge to the preparation of the food she set before us, and took as much pride in the results of her skill as an inventor takes in his appliances. And such wholesome, delicious, well-cooked dishes I have never eaten elsewhere. Clytia believed in intelligently prepared food, as she believed in intelligent instruction for her children; she would have thought it a crime to set an ignorant person over her kitchen.

And this woman of whom I am speaking knew that she held a place of honor and trust, and she filled it not only with dignity but lovingness. She had some younger women to assist her, whom she was instructing in the science and the art of cooking, and who would by-and-by take responsible positions themselves. These women, or girls, assisted also in the housekeeping, which was the most perfect system in point of cleanliness, order and beauty that it is possible to conceive of in a home; because skill, honesty and conscientiousness enter into every detail of the life of these people. The body is held in honor, and its needs are respected. Life is sacred, and physical sins, — neglect or infringement of the laws of health, — are classed in the same category with moral transgressions. In fact, the same principles and the same mathematical rules apply in the Three Natures of Man, — refined of course to correspond with the ascending scale from the lowest to the highest, from the physical to the spiritual. But so closely are the Three allied that there are no dividing lines, — there is no point where the Mind may say, "Here my responsibility ends," or where the Body may affirm, "I have only myself to please." Day by day these truths became clear to me. There was nothing particularly new in anything that I heard, — indeed it was all singularly familiar, in sound. But the wonder was, that the things we idealize, and theorize about, they accept literally, and absorb into their lives. They have made living facts of our profoundest philosophy and our sublimest poetry. Are we then too philosophical, too poetical, — and not practical? A good many centuries have rolled up their records and dropped them into eternity since we were given the simple, wonderful lesson, "Whatsoever a man sows that shall he also reap," — and we have not learned it yet! St. Paul's voice rings through the Earth from age to age, "Work out your own salvation," and we do not comprehend. These people have never had a Christ — in flesh and blood — but they have put into effect every precept of our Great Teacher. They have received the message, from whence I know not, — or rather by what means I know not, — "A new commandment I give unto you, that ye love one another."

# CHAPTER 10.

## THE MASTER.

> "I spoke as I saw.
> I report, as a man may report God's work—all's Love,
> yet all's Law."—BROWNING.

I have spoken of Ariadne, and promised to re-introduce her to you. You will remember her as the graceful girl who accompanied Clytia and her husband to Thursia. She had not made quite so strong an impression upon me as had the elder woman, perhaps because I was so preoccupied with, and interested in watching the latter's meeting with Elodia. Certainly there was nothing in the young woman herself, as I speedily ascertained, to justify disparagement even with Clytia. I was surprised to find that she was a member of our charming household.

She was an heiress; but she taught in one of the city schools, side by side with men and women who earned their living by teaching. I rather deprecated this fact in conversation with Clytia one day; I said that it was hardly fair for a rich woman to come in and usurp a place which rightfully belonged to some one who needed the work as a means of support,—alas! that I should have presumed to censure anything in that wonderful country. With knowledge came modesty.

Clytia's cheeks crimsoned with indignation. "Our teachers are not beneficiaries," she replied; "nor do we regard the positions in our schools — the teachers' positions — as charities to be dispensed to the needy. The profession is the highest and most honorable in our land, and only those who are fitted by nature and preparation presume to aspire to the office. There is no bar against those who are so fitted, — the richest and the most distinguished stand no better, and no poorer, chance than the poorest and most insignificant. We must have the best material, wherever it can be found."

We had but just entered the house, Clytia and I, when Ariadne glided down the stairs into the room where we sat, and approached me with the charming frankness and unaffectedness of manner which so agreeably characterizes the manners of all these people. She was rather tall, and slight; though her form did not suggest frailty. She resembled some elegant flower whose nature it is to be delicate and slender. She seemed even to sway a little, and undulate, like a lily on its stem.

I regarded her with attention, not unmixed with curiosity, — as a man is prone to regard a young lady into whose acquaintance he has not yet made inroads.

My chief impression about her was that she had remarkable eyes. They were of an indistinguishable, dark color, large horizontally but not too wide open, — eyes that drew yours continually, without your being able to tell whether it was to settle the question of color, or to find out the secret of their fascination, or whether it was simply that they appealed to your artistic sense — as being something finer than you had ever seen before. They were heavily fringed at top and bottom, and so were in shadow except when she raised them toward the light. Her complexion was pale, her hair light and fluffy; her brows and lashes were several shades darker than the hair. Her hands were lovely. Her dress was of course white, or cream, of some soft, clinging material; and she wore a bunch of blue flowers in her belt, slightly wilted.

There is this difference in women: some produce an effect simply, and others make a clear-cut, cameo-like impression upon the mind. Ariadne was of the latter sort. Whatever she appropriated, though but a tiny blossom, seemed immediately to proclaim its ownership and to swear its allegiance to her. From the moment I first saw her there, the blue flowers in her belt gave her, in my mind, the supreme title to all of their kind. I could never bear to see another woman wear the same variety, — and I liked them best when they were a little wilted! Her belongings suggested herself so vividly that if one came unexpectedly upon a fan, a book, a garment of hers, he was affected as by a presence.

I soon understood why it was that my eyes sought her face so persistently, drawn by a power infinitely greater than the mere power of beauty; it was due to the law of moral gravitation, — that by which men are attracted to a leader, through intuitive perception of a quality in him round which their own energies may nucleate. We all recognize the need of a centre, of a rallying-point, — save perhaps the few eccentrics, detached particles who have lost their place in the general order, makers of chaos and disturbers of peace.

It is this power which constitutes one of the chief qualifications of a teacher in Lunismar, because it rests upon a fact universally believed in, — spiritual royalty; an august force which cannot be ignored, and is never ridiculed — as Galileo was ridiculed, and punished, for his wisdom; because there ignorance and prejudice do not exist, and the superstition which planted the martyr's stake has never been known.

Ariadne said that she had been up in the observatory, and that there were indications of an approaching storm.

"I hope it may be a fine one!" exclaimed Clytia.

I thought this rather an extraordinary remark — coming from one of the sex whose formula is more likely to be, "I hope it will not be a severe one."

At that moment a man appeared in the doorway, the majesty of whose presence I certainly felt before my eyes fell upon him. Or it might have been the reflection I saw in the countenances of my two companions, — I stood with my back to the door, facing them, — which gave me the curious, awe-touched sensation.

I turned round, and Clytia immediately started forward. Ariadne exclaimed in an undertone, with an accent of peculiar sweetness, — a commingling of delight, and reverence, and caressing tenderness:

"Ah! the Master!"

Clytia took him by the hand and brought him to me, where I stood rooted to my place.

"Father, this is our friend," she said simply, without further ceremony of introduction. It was enough. He had come on purpose to see me, and therefore he knew who I was. As for him — one does not explain a king! The title by which Ariadne had called him did not at the moment raise an inquiry in my mind. I accepted it as the natural definition of the man. He was a man of kingly proportions, with eyes from which Clytia's had borrowed their limpid blackness. His glance had a wide compresiveness, and a swift, sure, loving insight.

He struck me as a man used to moving among multitudes, with his head above all, but his heart embracing all.

You may think it strange, but I was not abashed. Perfect love casteth out fear; and there was in this divine countenance — I may well call it divine! — the lambent light of a love so kindly and so tender, that fear, pride, vanity, egotism, even false modesty — our pet hypocrisy — surrendered without a protest.

I think I talked more than any one else, being delicately prompted to furnish some account of the world to which I belong, and stimulated by the profound interest with which the Master attended to every word that I said. But I received an equal amount of information myself, — usually in response to the questions with which I rounded up my periods, like this: We do so, and so, upon the Earth; how is it here? The replies threw an extraordinary light upon the social order and conditions there.

I naturally dwelt upon the salient characteristics of our people, — I mean, of course, the American people. I spoke of our enormous grasp of the commercial principle; of our manipulation of political and even social forces to great financial ends; of our easy acquisition of fortunes; of our tremendous push and energy, directed to the accumulation of wealth. And of our enthusiasms, and institutions; our religions and their antagonisms, and of the many other things in which we take pride.

And I learned that in Caskia there is no such thing as speculative enterprise. All business has an actual basis most discouraging to the adventurous spirit in search of sudden riches. There is no monetary skill worthy the dignified appellation of financial management, — and no use for that particular development of the talent of ingenuity.

All the systems involving the use of money conduct their affairs upon the simplest arithmetical rules in their simplest form; addition, subtraction, multiplication, division. There are banks, of course, for the mutual convenience of all, but there are no

magnificent delusions called "stocks;" no boards of trade, no
bulls and bears, no "corners," no mobilizing of capital for any
questionable purposes; no gambling houses; no pitfalls for un-
wary feet; and no mad fever of greed and scheming coursing
through the veins of men and driving them to insanity and self-
destruction. More than all, there are no fictitious values put upon
fads and fancies of the hour, — nor even upon works of art. The
Caskians are not easily deceived. An impostor is impossible. Because the people are instructed in the quality of things intellectual, and moral, and spiritual, as well as in things physical. They
are as sure of the knowableness of art, as they are — and as we
are — of the knowableness of science. Art is but refined science,
and the principles are the same in both, but more delicately, and
also more comprehensively, interpreted in the former than in
the latter.

One thing more: there are no would-be impostors. The law
operates no visible machinery against such crimes, should there
be any. The Master explained it to me in this way:

"The Law is established in each individual conscience, and
rests securely upon self-respect."

"Great heavens!" I cried, as the wonder of it broke upon my
understanding, "and how many millions of years has it taken your
race to attain to this perfection?"

"It is not perfection," he replied, "it only approximates perfection; we are yet in the beginning."

"Well, by the grace of God, you are on the right way!" said
I. "I am familiar enough with the doctrines you live by, to know
that it is the right way; they are the same that we have been taught,
theoretically, for centuries, but, to tell the truth, I never believed
they could be carried out literally, as you appear to carry them
out. We are tolerably honest, as the word goes, but when hon-

esty shades off into these hair-splitting theories, why—we leave
it to the preachers, and—women."

"Then you really have some among you who believe in the
higher truths?" the Master said, and his brows went up a little
in token of relief.—My picture of Earth-life must have seemed
a terrible one to him!

"O, yes, indeed," said I, taking my cue from this. And I proceeded to give some character sketches of the grand men and
women of Earth whose lives have been one long, heroic struggle
for truth, and to whom a terrible death has often been the crown-
ing triumph of their faith. I related to him briefly the history
of America from its discovery four hundred years ago; and told
him about the splendid material prosperity,—the enormous
wealth, the extraordinary inventions, the great population, the
unprecedented free-school system, and the progress in general
education and culture,—of a country which had its birth but
yesterday in a deadly struggle for freedom of conscience; and
of our later, crueller war for freedom that was not for ourselves
but for a despised race. I described the prodigious waves of public and private generosity that have swept millions of dollars into
burned cities for their rebuilding, and tons of food into famine-
stricken lands for the starving.

I told him of the coming together in fellowship of purpose,
of the great masses, to face a common danger, or to meet a common necessity; and of the moral and intellectual giants who in
outward appearance and in the seeming of their daily lives are
not unlike their fellows, but to whom all eyes turn for help and
strength in the hour of peril. But I did not at that time under-
take any explanation of our religious creeds, for it somehow
seemed to me that these would not count for much with a people
who expressed their theology solely by putting into practice the

things they believed. I had the thought in mind though, and determined to exploit it later on. As I have said before, the Master listened with rapt attention, and when I had finished, he exclaimed,

"I am filled with amazement! a country yet so young, so far advanced toward Truth!"

He gave himself up to contemplation of the picture I had drawn, and in the depths of his eyes I seemed to see an inspired prophecy of my country's future grandeur.

Presently he rose and went to a window, and, with uplifted face, murmured in accents of the sublimest reverence that have ever touched my understanding, "O, God, All-Powerful!"

And a wonderful thing happened: the invocation was responded to by a voice that came to each of our souls as in a flame of fire, "Here am I." The velocity of worlds is not so swift as was our transition from the human to the divine.

But it was not an unusual thing, this supreme triumph of the spirit; it is what these people call "divine worship,"—a service which is never perfunctory, which is not ruled by time or place. One may worship alone, or two or three, or a multitude, it matters not to God, who only asks to be worshiped in spirit and in truth,—be the time Sabbath or mid-week, the place temple, or field, or closet.

A little later I remarked to the Master,—wishing to have a point cleared up,—

"You say there are no fictitious values put upon works of art; how do you mean?"

He replied, "Inasmuch as truth is always greater than human achievement—which at best may only approximate the truth,—the value of a work of art should be determined by its merit alone, and not by the artist's reputation, or any other remote influence, — of course I do not include particular objects consecrated by association or by time. But suppose a man paints a great picture, for which he receives a great price, and thereafter uses the fame he has won as speculating capital to enrich himself, — I beg the pardon of every artist for setting up the hideous hypothesis! — But to complete it: the moment a man does that, he loses his self-respect, which is about as bad as anything that can happen to him; it is moral suicide. And he has done a grievous wrong to art by lowering the high standard he himself helped to raise. But his crime is no greater than that of the name-worshipers, who, ignorantly, or insolently, set up false standards and scorn the real test of values. However, these important matters are not left entirely to individual consciences; artists, and so-called art-critics, are not the only judges of art. We have no mysterious sanctuaries for a privileged few; all may enter, — all are indeed made to enter, not by violence, but by the simple, natural means employed in all teaching. All will not hold the brush, or the pen, or the chisel; but from their earliest infancy our children are carefully taught to recognize the forms of truth in all art; the eye was made to see, the ear to hear, the mind to understand."

The visit was at an end. When he left us it was as though the sun had passed under a cloud.

Clytia went out with him, her arm lovingly linked in his; and I turned to Ariadne. "Tell me," I said, "why is he called Master? Is it a formal title, or was it bestowed in recognition of the quality of the man?"

"Both," she answered. "No man receives the title who has not the 'quality.' But it is in one way perfunctory; it is the distinguishing title of a teacher of the highest rank."

"And what are teachers of the highest rank, presidents of colleges?" I asked.

"O, no," she replied with a smile, "they are not necessarily teachers of schools — old and young alike are their pupils. They are those who have advanced the farthest in all the paths of knowledge, especially the moral and the spiritual."

"I understand," said I; "they are your priests, ministers, pastors, — your Doctors of Divinity."

"Perhaps," she returned, doubtfully; our terminology was not always clear to those people.

"Usually," she went on, "they begin with teaching in the schools, — as a kind of apprenticeship. But, naturally, they rise; there is that same quality in them which forces great poets and painters to high positions in their respective fields."

"Then they rank with geniuses!" I exclaimed, and the mystery of the man in whose grand company I had spent the past hour was solved.

Ariadne looked at me as though surprised that I should have been ignorant of so natural and patent a fact.

"Excuse me!" said I, "but it is not always the case with us; any man may set up for a religious teacher who chooses, with or without preparation, — just as any one may set up for a poet, or a painter, or a composer of oratorio."

"Genius must be universal on your planet then," she returned innocently. I suppose that I might have let it pass, there was nobody to contradict any impressions I might be pleased to convey! but there is something in the atmosphere of Lunismar which compels the truth, good or bad.

"No," said I, "they do it by grace of their unexampled self-trust, — a quality much encouraged among us, — and because we do not legislate upon such matters. The boast of our country is liberty, and in some respects we fail to comprehend the glorious possession. Too often we mistake lawlessness for liberty.

The fine arts are our playthings, and each one follows his own fancy, like children with toys."

"Follows-his-own-fancy," she repeated, as one repeats a strange phrase, the meaning of which is obscure.

"By the way," I said, "you must be rather arbitrary here. Is a man liable to arrest or condign punishment, if he happens to burlesque any of the higher callings under the impression that he is a genius?"

She laughed, and I added, "I assure you that this is not an uncommon occurrence with us."

"It would be impossible here," she replied, "because no one could so mistake himself, though it seems egotistical for one of us to say so! but"—a curious expression touched her face, a questioning, doubting, puzzled look—"we are speaking honestly, are we not?"

I wondered if I had betrayed my American characteristic of hyperbole, and I smiled as I answered her:

"My countrymen are at my mercy, I know; but had I a thousand grudges against them, I beg you to believe that I am not so base as to take advantage of my unique opportunity to do them harm! We are a young people, as I said awhile ago, a very young people; and in many respects we have the innocent audacity of babes. Yes," I added, "I have told you the truth,—but not all of it; Earth, too, is pinnacled with great names,—of Masters, like yours, and poets, and painters, and scientists, and inventors. Even in the darkest ages there have been these points of illumination. What I chiefly wonder at here, is the universality of intelligence, of understanding. You are a teacher of children, pray tell me how you teach. How do you get such wonderful results? I can comprehend—a little—'what' you people are, I wish to know the 'how,' the 'why'."

"All our teaching," she said, "embraces the three-fold nature. The physical comes first of course, for you cannot reach the higher faculties through barriers of physical pain and sickness, hunger and cold. The child must have a good body, and to this end he is taught the laws that govern his body, through careful and attentive observance of cause and effect. And almost immediately, he begins to have fascinating glimpses of similar laws operating upon a higher than the physical plane. Children have boundless curiosity, you know, and this makes the teacher's work easy and delightful, — for we all love to tell a piece of news! Through this faculty, the desire to know, you can lead a child in whatever paths you choose. You can almost make him what you choose. A little experience teaches a child that every act brings consequences, good or bad; but he need not get all his knowledge by experience, that is too costly. The reasoning faculty must be aroused, and then the conscience, — which is to the soul what the sensatory nerves are to the body. But the conscience is a latent faculty, and here comes in the teacher's most delicate and important work. Conscience is quite dependent upon the intellect; we must know what is right and what is wrong, otherwise conscience must stagger blindly."

"Yes, I know," I interrupted, "the consciences of some very good people in our world have burned witches at the stake."

"Horrible!" she said with a shudder.

She continued: "This, then, is the basis. We try, through that simple law of cause and effect, which no power can set aside, to supply each child with a safe, sure motive for conduct that will serve him through life, as well in his secret thought as in outward act. No one with this principle well-grounded in him will ever seek to throw the blame of his misdeeds upon another. We teach the relative value of repentance; that though it cannot avert or annul the effects of wrong-doing, it may serve to prevent repetition of the wrong."

"Do you punish offenders?" I asked.

She smiled. "Punishment for error is like treating symptoms instead of the disease which produced them, is it not? — relief for the present, but no help for the future. Punishment, and even criticism, are dangerous weapons, to be used, if at all, with a tact and skill that make one tremble to think of! They are too apt to destroy freedom of intercourse between teacher and pupil. Unjust criticism, especially, shuts the teacher from an opportunity to widen the pupil's knowledge. Too often our criticisms are barriers which we throw about ourselves, shutting out affection and confidence; and then we wonder why friends and family are sealed books to us!"

"That is a fact," I assented, heartily, "and no one can keep to his highest level is he is surrounded by an atmosphere of coldness and censure. Even Christ, our Great Teacher, affirmed that he could not do his work in certain localities because of prevailing unbelief."

"There is one thing which it is difficult to learn," went on Ariadne, "discrimination, the fitness of things. I may not do that which is proper for another to do, — why? Because in each individual consciousness is a special and peculiar law of destiny upon which rests the burden of personal responsibility. It is this law of the individual that makes it an effrontery for any one to constitute himself the chancellor of another's conscience, or to sit in judgment upon any act which does not fall under the condemnation of the common law. It is given to each of us to create a world, — within ourselves and round about us, — each unlike all the others, though conforming to the universal principles of right, as poets, however original, conform to the universal principles of language. We have choice — let me give you a paradox! — every one may have first choice of inexhaustible material in infinite variety. But how to choose!"

I quoted Milton's lines:

> "He that has light within his own clear breast,
> May sit in the center and enjoy bright day;
> But he that hides a dark soul and foul thoughts,
> Benighted walks under the mid-day sun;
> Himself is his own dungeon."

She thanked me with a fine smile.

Clytia had come in a few moments before, but her entrance had been such that it had caused no disturbing vibrations in the current of sympathetic understanding upon which Ariadne and myself were launched.

Now, however, we came ashore as it were, and she greeted us as returned voyagers love to be greeted, with cordial welcome.

She informed us that dinner was ready, and I was alarmed lest we might have delayed that important function.

The children had disappeared for the day, having already had their dinner in the nursery under the supervision of their mother.

Calypso had invited in his friend Fides. He was a man of powerful frame, and strong, fine physiognomy; with a mind as virile as the former, and as clear-cut as the latter. The woman who had created the dinner — I do not know of a better word — also sat at table with us, and contributed many a gem to the thought of the hour. Thought may seem an odd word to use in connection with a dinner conversation, — unless it is a 'toast' dinner! but even in their gayest and lightest moods these people are never thoughtless. Their minds instead of being lumbering machinery requiring much force and preparation to put in motion, are set upon the daintiest and most delicate wheels. Their mental equipment corresponds with the astonishing mechanical contrivances for overcoming friction in the physical world. And this exquisite machinery is applied in exactly the same ways, — sometimes for utility, and sometimes for simple enjoyment.

Ariadne's prediction had been correct, the storm-king was mustering his forces round the mountain-tops, and the Eudosa was answering the challenge from the valley.

After dinner we went up into the observatory, and from thence passed out onto the balcony, thrilled by the same sense of delightful expectancy you see in the unennuied eyes of Youth, waiting for the curtain to go up at a play. All save myself had of course seen thunder-storms in Lunismar, but none were *blasé.* There was eagerness in every face.

We took our station at a point which gave us the best view of the mountains, and saw the lightning cut their cloud-enwrapped sides with flaming swords, and thrust gleaming spears down into the darkling valley, as if in furious spite at the blackness which had gathered everywhere. For the sun had sunk behind a wall as dense as night and left the world to its fate. Before the rain began to fall there was an appalling stillness, which even the angry mutterings of the Eudosa could not overcome. And then, as though the heavens had marshaled all their strength for one tremendous assault, the thunder broke forth. I have little physical timidity, but the shock struck me into a pose as rigid as death.

The others were only profoundly impressed, spiritually alive to the majesty of the performance.

That first explosion was but the prelude to the mighty piece played before us, around us, at our feet, and overhead.

Earth has been spared the awfulness — (without destruction) — and has missed the glory of such a storm as this.

But the grandest part was yet to come. The rain lasted perhaps twenty minutes, and then a slight rent was made in the thick and sombre curtain that covered the face of the heavens, and a single long shaft of light touched the frozen point of the Spear and turned its crystal and its snow to gold. The rest of the mountain was still swathed in cloud. A moment more, and a superb rainbow, and another, and yet another, were flung upon the shoulder of the Spear, below the glittering finger. The rent in the curtain grew wider, and beyond, all the splendors of colors were blazoned upon the shimmering draperies that closed about and slowly vanished with the sun.

We sat in silence for a little time. I happened to be near Fides, and I presently turned to him and said:

"That was a most extraordinary manifestation of the Almighty's power!"

He looked at me but did not reply.

Ariadne, who had heard my remark, exclaimed laughingly:

"Fides thinks the opening of a flower is a far more wonderful manifestation than the stirring up of the elements!"

In the midst of the storm I had discovered the Master standing at the farther end of the balcony, and beside him a tall, slender woman with thick, white hair, whom I rightly took to be his wife. I was presented to her shortly, and the mental comment I made at the moment, I never afterward reversed, — "She is worthy to be the Master's wife!"

Although the rain had ceased, the sky was a blank, as night settled upon the world. Not a star shone. But it was cool and pleasant, and we sat and talked for a couple of hours. Suddenly, a band of music on the terrace below silenced our voices. It was most peculiar music: now it was tone-pictures thrown upon the dark background of shadows; and now it was a dance of sprites; and now a whispered confidence in the ear. It made no attempt to arouse the emotions, to produce either sadness or exaltation. It was a mere frolic of music. When it was over, I went down stairs, with the others, humming an inaudible tune, as though I had been to the opera.

# CHAPTER 11.

### A COMPARISON.

"He who rests on what he is, has a destiny above destiny, and can make mouths at fortune."—EMERSON.

"Work out your own salvation."—ST. PAUL.

I had a feeling, when I retired to my room that night, as if years lay between me and the portion of my life which I had spent in Paleveria. But across the wide gulf my soul embraced Severnius. All that was beautiful, and lovable, and noble in that far-off country centered in him, as light centres in a star.

But of Elodia I could not think without pain. I even felt a kind of helpless rage mingling with the pain,—remembering that it was simply the brutality of the social system under which she had been reared, that had stamped so hideous a brand upon a character so fair. I contrasted her in my mind with the women asleep in the rooms about me, whose thoughts were as pure as the thoughts of a child. Had she been born here, I reflected, she would have been like Clytia, like Ariadne. And oh! the pity of it, that she had not!

I was restless, wakeful, miserable, thinking of her; remembering her wit, her intelligence, her power; remembering how charming she was, how magnetic, and alas! how faulty!

She gave delight to all about her, and touched all life with color. But she was like a magnificent bouquet culled from the gardens of wisdom and beauty; a thing of but temporary value, whose fragrance must soon be scattered, whose glory must soon pass away.

Ariadne was the white and slender lily, slowly unfolding petal after petal in obedience to the law of its own inner growth. Should the blossom be torn asunder its perfume would rise as incense about its destroyer, and from the life hidden at its root would come forth more perfect blossoms and more delicate fragrance.

I had arrived at this estimate of her character by a process more unerring and far swifter than reason. You might call it spiritual telegraphy. The thought of her not only restored but immeasurably increased my faith in woman; and I fell asleep at last soothed and comforted.

I awoke in the morning to the sound of singing. It was Ariadne's voice, and she was touching the strings of a harp. All Caskians sing, and all are taught to play upon at least one musical instrument. Every household is an orchestra.

Ariadne's voice was exceptionally fine — where all voices were excellent. Its quality was singularly bird-like; sometimes it was the joyous note of the lark, and again it was the tenderly sweet, and passionately sad, dropping-song of the mocking-bird.

When I looked out of my window, the sun was just silvering the point of the Spear, and light wreaths of mist were lifting from the valleys. I saw the Master, staff in hand, going up toward the mountains, and Fides was coming across the hills.

I had wondered, when I saw the Master and his wife on the balcony the night before, how they came to be there at such an hour on such a night. I took the first opportunity to find out. The only way to find out about people's affairs in Caskia, is by asking questions, or, by observation — which takes longer. They speak with their lives instead of their tongues, concerning so many things that other people are wordy about. They are quite devoid of theories. But they are charmingly willing to impart what one wishes to know.

I learned that Clytia's parents lived within a stone's throw of her house on one side, and Calypso's grandparents at about the same distance on the other. And I also learned that it was an arrangement universally practiced; the clustering together of families, in order that the young might always be near at hand to support, and protect, and to smooth the pathway of the old. Certain savage races upon the Earth abandon the aged to starvation and death; certain other races, not savage, abandon them to a loneliness that is only less cruel. But these extraordinarily just people repay to the helplessness of age, the tenderness and care, the loving sympathy, which they themselves received in the helplessness of infancy.

The grandparents happened to be away from home, and I did not meet them for some days.

On that first morning we had Clytia's parents to breakfast. Immediately after breakfast the circle broke up. It was Clytia's morning to visit and assist in the school which her little ones attended; Ariadne started off to her work, with a fresh cluster of the delicious blue flowers in her belt; and I had the choice of visiting the steel-works with Calypso, or taking a trip to Lake Eudosa, on foot, with the Master. I could hardly conceal the delight with which I decided in favor of the latter. We set off at once, and what a walk it was! A little way through the city, and then across a strip of lush green meadow, starred with daisies, thence into sweet-smelling woods, and then down, down, down, along the rocky edge of the canyon, past the deafening waterfalls to the wonderful Lake!

We passed, on our way through the city, a large, fine structure which, upon inquiry, I found to be the place where the Master "taught" on the Sabbath day.

"Do you wish to look in?" he asked, and we turned back and entered. The interior was beautiful and vast, capacious enough to seat several thousand people; and every Sunday it was filled.

I thought it a good opportunity for finding out something about the religion of this people, and I began by asking:

"Are there any divisions in your Church, — different denominations, I mean?"

He seemed unable to comprehend me, and I was obliged to enter into an explanation, which I made as simple as possible, of course, relative to the curse of Adam and the plan of redemption. In order that he might understand the importance attaching to our creeds, I told him of the fierce, sanguinary struggles of past ages, and the grave controversies of modern times, pertaining to certain dogmas and tenets, — as to whether they were essential, or nonessential to salvation.

"Salvation from what?" he asked.

"Why, from sin."

"But how? We know only one way to be saved from sin."

"And what is that?" I inquired.

"Not to sin."

"But that is impossible!" I rejoined, feeling that he was trifling with the subject. Though that was unlike him.

"Yes, it is impossible," he replied, gravely. "God did not make us perfect. He left us something to do for ourselves."

"That is heretical," said I. "Don't you believe in the Fall of Man?"

"No, I think I believe in the Rise of Man," he answered, smiling.

"O, I keep forgetting," I exclaimed, "that I am on another planet!"

"And that this planet has different relations with God from what your planet has?" returned he. "I cannot think so, sir; it is altogether a new idea to me, and—pardon me!—an illogical one. We belong to the same system, and why should not the people of Mars have the sentence for sin revoked, as well as the people of Earth? Why should not we have been provided with an intercessor? But tell me, is it really so?—do you upon the Earth not suffer the consequences of your acts?"

"Why, certainly we do," said I; "while we live. The plan of salvation has reference to the life after death."

He dropped his eyes to the ground.

"You believe in that life, do you not?" I asked.

"Believe in it!"—he looked up, amazed. "All life is eternal; as long as God lives, we shall live."

A little later he said:

"You spoke of the fall of man,—what did you mean?"

"That Man was created a perfect being, but through sin became imperfect, so that God could not take him back to Himself,—save by redemption."

"And God sent His Only Son to the Earth, you say, to redeem your race from the consequences of their own acts?"

"So we believe," said I.

After another brief silence, he remarked:

"Man did not begin his life upon this planet in perfection."

At this moment we passed a beautiful garden, in which there was an infinite profusion of flowers in infinite variety.

"Look at those roses!" he exclaimed; "God planted the species, a crude and simple plant, and turned it over to man to do what he might with it; and in the same way he placed man himself here, — to perfect himself if he would. I am not jealous of God, nor envious of you; but just why He should have arranged to spare you all this labor, and commanded us to work out our own salvation, I cannot comprehend."

It struck me as a remarkable coincidence that he should have used the very words of one of our own greatest logicians.

A longer silence followed. The Master walked with his head inclined, in the attitude of profound thought. At last he drew a deep breath and looked up, relaxing his brows.

"It may be prodigiously presumptuous," he said, "but I am inclined to think there has been a mistake somewhere."

"How, a mistake?" I asked.

He paid no heed to the question, but said: "Tell me the story, — tell me the exact words, if you can, of this Great Teacher whom you believe to be the Son of God?"

I gave a brief outline of the Saviour's life and death, and it was a gratification to me — because it seemed, in some sort, an acknowledgment, or concession to my interpretation, — to see that he was profoundly affected.

"Oh!" he cried, — his hands were clenched and his body writhed as with the actual sufferings of the Man of Sorrows, — "that a race of men should have been brought through such awful tribulation to see God! Why could they not accept the truth from his lips?"

"Because they would not. They kept crying 'Give us a sign,' and he gave himself to death."

I grouped together as many of the words of Christ as I could recall, and I was surprised, not only that his memory kept its grasp on them all, but that he was able to see at once their innermost meaning. It was as if he dissolved them in the wonderful alembic of his understanding, and instantly restored them in crystals of pure truth, divested alike of mysticism and remote significance. He took them up, one by one, and held them to the light, as one holds precious gems. He knew them, recognized them, and appraised them with the delight, and comprehensiveness, and the critical judgment of a connoisseur of jewels.

"You believe that Christ came into your world," he said, "that you 'might have life.' That is, he came to teach you that the life of the soul, and not the body, is the real life. He died 'that you might live,' but it was not the mere fact of his death that assured your life. He was willing to give up his life in pledge of the truth of what he taught, that you might believe that truth, and act upon that belief, and so gain life. He taught only the truth, — his soul was a fountain of truth. Hence, when he said, Suffer the little children to come unto me, it was as though he said, Teach your children the truths I have taught you. And when he cried in the tenderness of his great and yearning love, Come unto me all ye that labor and are heavy laden, and I will give you rest, he meant, — oh! you cannot doubt it, my friend, — he meant, Come, give up your strifes, and hatreds, your greeds, and vanities, and selfishness, and the endless weariness of your pomps and shows; come to me and learn how to live, and where to find peace, and contentment. 'A new commandment I give unto you, that ye love one another.' This was the 'easy yoke,' and the 'light burden,' which your Christ offered to you in place of the tyranny of sin. 'Whatsoever ye would that men should do to you, do ye even so to them.' There is nothing finer than that, — there is no law above that! We Caskians have been trying to work upon that principle for thousands of years. It is all that there is of religion, save the spiritual perception of abstract truths which we may conceive of, more or less clearly, as attributes of God. Your Great Teacher explained to you that God is a spirit, and should be worshiped in spirit and in truth. Hence we may worship Him where and when we will. Worship is not a ceremony, but profound contemplation of the infinite wisdom, and infinite power, and the infinite love of God. The outdoor world, — here, where we stand now, with the marvelous sky above us, the clouds, the sun; this mighty cataract before us; and all the teeming life, the beauty, the fragrance, the song, — is the best place of all. I pity the man who lacks the faculty of worship! it means that though he may have eyes he sees not, and ears he hears not."

"Do you believe in temples of worship?" I asked.

"Yes," he replied, "I believe in them; for though walls and stained windows shut out the physical glories of the world, they do not blind the eyes of the spirit. And if there is one in the pulpit who has absorbed enough of the attributes of God into his soul to stand as an interpreter to the people, it is better than waiting outside. Then, too, there is grandeur in the coming together of a multitude to worship in oneness of spirit. And all things are better when shared with others. I believe that art should bring its best treasures to adorn the temples of worship, and that music should voice this supreme adoration. But in this matter, we should be careful not to limit God in point of locality. What does the saying mean, 'I asked for bread, and ye gave me a stone?' I think it might mean, for one thing, 'I asked where to find God, and you pointed to a building.' The finite mind is prone to worship its own creations of God. There are ignorant races upon this planet, — perhaps also upon yours, — who dimly recognize Deity in this way; they bring the best they have of skill in handiwork, to the making of a pitiful image to represent God; and then, forgetting the motive, they bow down to the image. We call that idolatry. But it is hard even for the enlightened to avoid this sin."

He paused a moment and then went on:

"I cannot comprehend the importance you seem to place upon the forms and symbols, nor in what way they relate to religion, but they may have some temporary value, I can hardly judge of that. Baptism, you say, is a token and a symbol, but do a people so far advanced in intelligence and perception, still require tokens and symbols? And can you not, even yet, separate the spiritual meaning of Christ's words from their literal meaning? You worship the man — the God, if you will, — instead of that for which he stood. He himself was a symbol, he stood for the things he wished to teach. 'I am the truth,' 'I am the life.' Do you not see that he meant, 'I am the exponent of truth, I teach you how to live; hearken unto me.' In those days in which he lived, perhaps, language was still word-pictures, and the people whom he taught could not grasp the abstract, hence he used the more forcible style, the concrete. He could not have made this clearer, than in those remarkable words, 'Inasmuch as ye have done it unto one of the least of these, my brethren, ye have done it unto me.'"

"I know," I replied, as he paused for some response from me; "my intellect accepts your interpretation of these things, but this symbolic religion of ours is ingrained in our very consciences, so that neglect of the outward forms of christianity seems almost worse than actual sin."

"And it will continue to be so," he said, "until you learn to practice the truth for truth's sake, — until you love your neighbor — not only because Christ commanded it, but because the principle of love is 'ingrained in your consciences.' As for belonging to a church, I can only conceive of that in the social sense, for every soul that aspires upward belongs to Christ's church universal. They are the lambs of his flock, the objects of his tenderest care. But I can see how a great number of religious societies, or organizations, are possible, as corresponding with the requirements of different groups of people."

"Yes," I said, glad of this admission, "and these societies are all aiming at the same thing that you teach, — the brotherhood of man. They clothe the poor, they look after the sick, they send missionaries to the heathen, they preach morality and temperance, — all, in His Name, because, to tell the truth, they cannot conceive of any virtue disassociated from the man, Jesus. Jesus is the great leader of the spiritual forces marshaled under the banners of truth upon the Earth. In all their good works, which are so great and so many, good christians give Christ the glory, because, but for him, they would not have had the Truth, the Life, — the world was so dark, so ignorant. All the ancient civilizations upon the Earth, — and some of them were magnificent! — have perished, because they did not possess this truth and this spiritual life which Christ taught. There was a great deal of knowledge, but not love; there was a great deal of philosophy, but it was cold. There was mysticism, but it did not satisfy. Do you wonder, sir, that a world should love the man who brought love into that world, — who brought peace, good-will, to men?"

"No, no," said the Master, "I do not wonder. It is grand, sublime! And he gave his body to be destroyed by his persecutors, in order to prove to the world that there is a life higher than the physical, and indestructible, — and that physical death has no other agony than physical pain. Ah, I see, I understand, and I am not surprised that you call this man your redeemer! I think, my friend," he added, "that you have now a civilization upon the Earth, which will not perish!"

After a moment, he remarked, turning to me with a smile, "We are not so far apart as we thought we were, when we first started out, are we?"

"No," said I, "the only wonder to me is, that you should have been in possession, from the beginning, of the same truths that were revealed to us only a few centuries ago, through, as we have been taught to believe, special Divine Favor."

"Say, rather, Infinite Divine Love," he returned; "then we shall indeed stand upon the same plane, all alike, children of God."

As we continued our walk, his mind continued to dwell upon the teachings of Christ, and he sought to make clear to me one thing after another.

"Pray without ceasing," he repeated, reflectively. "Well, now, it would be impossible to take that literally; the literal meaning of prayer is verbal petition. The real meaning is, the sincere desire of the soul. You are commanded to pray in secret, and God will reward you openly. Put the two together and you have this: Desire constantly, within your secret soul, to learn and to practice the truth; and your open reward shall be the countless blessings which are attracted to the perfect life, the inner life. 'Ask whatsoever you will, in my name, and it shall be granted you.' That is, 'Ask in the name of truth and love.' Shall you pray for a personal blessing or favor which might mean disaster or injury to another? Prayer is the desire and effort of the soul to keep in harmony with God's great laws of the universe."

As it had been in Thursia, so it was here; people came to see me from all parts, and there were some remarkable companies in Clytia's parlors! Usually they were spontaneous gatherings, evening parties being often made up with little or no pre-meditation. There was music always, in great variety, and of the most delightful and elevated character, — singing, and many kinds of bands. And sometimes there was dancing, — not of the kind which awakened in De Quincey's soul, "the very grandest form of passionate sadness," — but of a kind that made me wish I had been the inventor of the phrase, "poetry of motion," so that I could have used it here, fresh and unhackneyed. In all, there was no more voluptuousness than in the frolic of children. Conversation might be — and often was — as light as the dance of butter-flies, but it was liable at any moment to rise, upon a hint, or a suggestion, to the most sublimated regions of thought, — for these people do not leave their minds at home when they go into society. And here, in society, I saw the workings of the principle of brotherly love, in a strikingly beautiful aspect. There was no disposition on the part of any one to outdo another; rather there seemed to be a general conspiracy to make each one rise to his best. The spirit of criticism was absent, and the spirit of petty jealousy. The women without exception were dressed with ex-quisite taste, because this is a part of their culture. And every woman was beautiful, for loving eyes approved her; and every man was noble, for no one doubted him.

If the sky was clear, a portion of each evening was spent in the observatory, or out upon the balcony, as the company chose, and the great telescope was always in requisition, and always pointed to the Earth! — if the Earth was in sight.

The last evening I spent in Lunismar was such a one as I have described. Ariadne and I happened to be standing together, and alone, in a place upon the balcony which commanded a view of our world. It was particularly clear and brilliant that night, and you may imagine with what feelings I contemplated it, being about to return to it! We had been silent for some little time, when she turned her eyes to me — those wonderful eyes! — and said, a little sadly, I thought:

"I shall never look upon Earth again, without happy memories of your brief visit among us."

A strange impulse seized me, and I caught her hands and held them fast in mine. "And I, O, Ariadne! when I return to Earth again, and lift my eyes toward heaven, it will not be Mars that I shall see, but only — Ariadne!"

A strange light suddenly flashed over her face and into her eyes as she raised them to mine, and in their clear depths was revealed to me the supreme law of the universe, the law of life, the law of love. In a voice tremulous with emotion — sad, but not hopeless — she murmured:

"And I, also, shall forget my studies in the starry fields of space to watch for your far-distant planet — the Earth — which shall forever touch all others with its glory."

And there, under the stars, with the plaintive music of the Eudosa in our ears, and seeing dimly through the darkness the white finger of the snowy peaks pointing upward, we looked into each other's eyes and — "I saw a new heaven and a new earth."

THE END